# TOO HARD TO HANDLE

# TOO HARD TO HANDLE

ANAMIKA MISHRA

KALPAZ

ISBN : 978-81-7835-994-6
₹ 250

First Published 2013

*Published by*

**Kalpaz Publications**
C-30, Satyawati Nagar,
Delhi-110052
Ph. : 9212142040
E-mail: kalpaz@hotmail.com

*Laser Typesetting* : Rudra Computer Graphics, Delhi
*Printed at* : G. Print Process, Delhi

**Cataloging in Publication Data—DK**
Courtesy: D.K. Agencies (P) Ltd. <docinfo@dkagencies.com>

**Mishra, Anamika.**
**Too Hard to Handle** / Anamika Mishra.
p. cm.
Novel.
ISBN 9788178359946

1. Indic fiction (English). I. Title.

DDC 823.92 23

## Dedicated Prayer

*Thank you God for the world so sweet,*
*Thank you God for the food we eat,*
*Thank you God for the birds that sing,*
*Thank you God for everything.*

**Amen**

Dear Family,
***I Love You...***

# Contents

# Preface

A little girl of class 4th, who wrote her first article for the school magazine on the topic– "Science– A boon or a bane" never thought, that she would become a writer and would get published her own novel, but that girl always had a faith that dreams do come true... She excelled in dancing, tried singing, learnt playing guitar, also tried her luck in academics did BCA and then MJMC. All the time she was trying to learn something new, she was actually exploring herself. She wrote about everything, either in her diary or in her blog!! One day, her mother and brother on reading her diary made her realise that she should stop exploring herself because she loves to write and that is all what she should do...

I really want to thank God for making my dream come true. Also heartly thanks to my brother Mr. Swapnil Mishra, who made me realise about what actually I am good at. Also would like to thank my Mom Mrs. Renu Mishra, who have been my inspiration since childhood as she herself use to write short stories in Hindi and English comic books and also Sir Paulo Coelho who inspired me as a writer. Special thanks to my Dad Mr. Shailendra Mishra for keeping up with my madness and teaching me precious lessons of life. Also to my bhabi, Mrs. Apsara Mishra for being there as a friend. Not to forget my childhood friend Harshit (Tintin) without whom this dream of mine would not have been possible and Neha Khare (my Roomy) for being my punching bag on many ocassions.

Big thanks to Kalpaz Publications, Delhi for their support and encouragement.

Thanks everyone for believing in my ability.

***This book is a tribute to my GrandPa Late Sh. R.N. Mishra and GrandMa Late Smt. Sarojani Devi Mishra.***

Finally, thank you God for making me your lucky child...

**Anamika**

# 1

# The World of Despair

*My eyes are wet, my legs are numb,*
*Sitting by the river with noise so dumb,*
*A silent noise is saying something,*
*My ears to hear that missing one thing,*
*So silent yet loud,*
*Like a crystal sky with intense cloud...*
*Nowhere to move, No way to go,*
*I might not be wrong if I say so,*
*Neither I left you, nor you left me,*
*Then what left us? That became 'I' from 'we'?*
*Please get me my smile back,*
*Which I have left many miles back,*
*Far away I have come from there,*
*A place which was full of love and care!!*
*Pain and grief all around me,*
*Loneliness is so much bound me!*
*Nowhere to move, No way to go,*
*I might not be wrong if I say so,*
*Neither I left you, nor you left me,*
*Then what left us? That became 'I' from 'we'?*

I looked at the sky and said, "Vivaan, please come back."

Tears came out of my eyes. I closed my eyes very tightly.

2 hours back...

"Anushree??? What am I hearing???" said Vivaan from the back.

Anushree turned back. She got freaked out as she saw Vivaan standing behind her.

"I was about to come to you only, Vivaan..." Anushree somehow managed to speak out of her fear.

"What is all this? Who is this guy? What was he saying to you?" asked Vivaan pointing towards a six feet tall fair man standing the other side of Anushree.

"Vivaan, I can explain you everything" – Anushree tried to stop Vivaan but he was moving away. She ran and stopped his way, by standing in front of him. But Vivaan pushed her aside and said, "It was my fault ... all my fault, that I trusted you... your innocence, your love... but to hell with all that!! You just don't deserve me!! I am right now breaking off with you. I never want to see your face. Good bye, Anushree!!"

Anushree burst into tears and said, "Vivaan, please don't go..."

I (Anushree) closed my eyes and shouted, 'Vivaan' and when opened back,

'It was a dream'.

I realised that I was sitting at the *Ganga Bairaj*, all alone by myself. Two hours have passed. Vivaan is gone now. I couldn't stop myself from bursting into tears again and again. I had lost someone whom I loved and was about to get married.

'But what went wrong? What was my fault?' I couldn't stop wondering this again and again.

Meanwhile I heard a voice - "Excuse me, madam!!"

I swept my tears and turned back. There was a very innocent looking girl and a witty-looking stud type's boy standing behind.

"Hmmm?" [I replied trying to hide my big swallowed eyes].

"Excuse me? Did you say anything?" exclaimed that girl.

"Naah! Nothing. I was just... ammm kind of... lost in dreams. Anyway, say? How can I help you?" I said to them rubbing my forehead with palms. I was trying to wipe the tear marks from my cheeks so that they couldn't see them.

"Ma'am, sorry to disturb you. Wanted to ask, are you Anushree Sharma?" asked that girl in excitement.

I replied, "yeah", managing to smile in front of them.

"Author of the novel *Before Saying Sorry?"* That boy confirmed.

"Yeah, why what happened?"

That girl with joy said to the guy standing beside her, "See I told you!"

"Ma'am, my name is Khushi and he is Ayush, my boyfriend" pointing towards the guy beside her.

"Well, can I have your autograph?" asked Khushi.

"Autograph??? I am hardly a celebrity!!" I rebutted.

Khushi tried to convince me with – "Ma'am, I really loved that novel. I also follow your blog on internet. You write really well. Plus, your photographs in that *Delhi Heights* magazine are just too fabulous!! I am your true fan. I know everything about you!!"

"Oh please. I don't think... I mean..." – I tried to answer.

But Khushi insisted taking out a pen and a paper from her bag – "Ma'am, pleeeeease...!!!!"

"Thanks for the appreciation dear!" I replied with a smile and signed her paper.

"Thank you so much!!" – Khushi said in joy.

Ayush was silent and was continuously gazing at me.

"Ma'am, if I am not wrong, today you are going to be awarded as the best debutant author of the year for your book?" – asked Ayush.

"Yeah!"

"So... aren't you attending that function (event) – Ayush"?

"I don't wanna talk about that!" I replied looking again towards the river and trying to ignore that couple.

"You don't look fine! Are you?" asked Khushi.

"Can we help you? You can share your problem with us", said Ayush.

"No thanks... I'll be fine!!" I said rudely.

"Ma'am, please! Treat us as a friend." said Ayush.

"It's OK, I am fine... just wanna be alone for some time!" - I was getting annoyed by their presence. I wanted to sit alone and cry my heart out. I don't need a friend or anyone at that very moment.

"Ok then, I think we should leave now. Thanks a lot, ma'am!" -Khushi replied.

I gave them a smile. Although it was hard to smile in that situation, but I somehow managed for that young and blessed couple.

"God bless you both! You guys are really lucky, touch wood...!!" I murmured to myself as I saw them going away.

They both were gone and soon she was back to loneliness.

I was gazing at the running water of the river Ganga, wondering what life would be if it wouldn't have been running so fast like this water. It would all have been stagnant. By then all would have got a lot of time to take decision... to judge whether a person is trustworthy or not... And may be to make ourselves more understandable and more transparent to others so that they don't misunderstand us...

For an ordinary person whose dream has come true, is happy in such a situation but for me, it was the most tragic day of my life. So much had happened since morning, it felt like the journey of ten years had contracted into this one whole day...

And in the end, he left me...

'Today is the day, when finally the most desired dream of mine would turn into reality. It was the day when I was to be awarded as the Best Debutant Author of the Year for my first book *Before Saying Sorry*.

The dream of standing on the podium, being appreciated for my hardwork with the award, which I decided would dedicate to my family, left incomplete...

Miss Destiny never favoured me. Only once it did, which changed my life forever... But that also lead me to loneliness today...

'She always wanted to be an author. But this first book of hers was not at all planned. It was just by an accident which made her an author before time else she had planned to write a book after gaining some experience in life. Who knew that her first book will be a book of confessions made by her, to the people in her life, a book of incomplete and unanswered questions left way back in the past years, a book of her life... life of a girl. And above all, who knew that this book would be loved and appreciated by all in this country'.

Everybody is happy for me, except me. Kanpur streets are full of hoardings for my book's success with my name and pictures. Credit, of course, goes to the advertisers and sponsors but when you see your hoardings and posters with titles like "Our City's Pride..." and all that, it really gives a heavenly feeling. More heavenly when I would have been on the stage to receive the award for my book and the hall echoed with the sound of claps and hoots of the people present there... media taking pictures and my thank you speech been written down... And all, just for me...

But Miss Destiny... and Mr. Luck......... What shall be said for them...

People say admitting the mistake and telling the truth leads to a stronger bond in a relationship. But in my case, it was just the inverse. I didn't even get a chance to explain what exactly truth was?

Why do philosophies never work for me!'

I might be sounding very depressing right now, but I was never like this before. Though being a very deep-thinker, I was on the other hand very childish. But with time, all the thoughts and perceptions of mine changed and took a new shape of maturity.

I always wonder... Life - A four letter word, so simple to pronounce, yet it is the most complex term of the whole dictionary. It is so weird that the happy times of your life always make you cry when you remember them. Sometimes you either wish to have a forward button to skip all your problems or you need a rewind button to go back in the past and rectify the mistakes done by you. Sometimes you have to decide what is more important for you in life - a relation or a truth of your life. Sometimes it's too beautiful that you wish to re-live each and every moment and sometimes every moment of your life is just too hard to handle..."

Right now, I am here sitting at the bank of River Ganga. It's actually a dam named *Ganga-Bairaj* situated at the outskirts of my home city - Kanpur.

Kanpur, apart from the reason that it is my home town, has always been special to me. A place where I feel known to all. A place which loves me and knows me. Six years of living in Delhi didn't do that magic on me and couldn't take Kanpur's place in my heart. And if talking about *Ganga-Bairaj*, it's a place where you can sit with yourself, connect yourself to your most inner-self, talk to the nature, listen to the sound of flowing water and feel the cool breeze.

You can sit here for hours and hours just watching the nature at its best. It's the most favourite place of mine. I used to come here very often with my daddy when I was 10. From that time I had fallen for this place, but I never thought that I will have a desire to visit this favourite place of mine on the most tragic day of my life.

There are times in your life when you feel like being all alone, feeling the loneliness, talking to yourself and crying your heart out loud.

He promised to never leave me alone and love me no matter what happens.

I never thought he would leave me... leave me just like that...

He must have shouted on me, argued with me, scolded me or even thrashed ... but why did he go away...

I saw a couple which passed right from my back. They were fighting with each other. The girl was shouting on the guy that you should have informed me..!!

The boy was saying sorry again and again but the girl wasn't listening to him. The girl threatened the boy that 'she will leave him forever...'.

I felt like going to them and telling them the pain of loosing someone in real... and stop them from fighting.

But they were also gone...

I remember, we often used to fight before.

But usually we had silly fights on small and stupid topics like eating non-veg is a bad thing, getting drenched in the rain is a pleasure to feel, Pepsi is better than Mirinda, Shahrukh Khan is better than Amir Khan, I write well and you don't, etc.

We never fought on serious matters like "why was your phone busy?" "Who was that guy?" "Who was that girl?" "Don't wear such clothes!!" and so on, like other couples do.

And all the time I fought with him I loved and enjoyed arguing on such matters.

This small incident of seeing a couple arguing, made me again realise that he has left me and I would never ever get a chance to fight with him like this again.

People say those who fight a lot are ones who love each other a lot.

But what exactly is love ?

People have so many definitions of love!!

And so do I ... not many but few... which are simple to understand.

Love is when you don't care about what you feel but care for and respect the feelings and values of your partner. Love is when you stay back by their side in all the good and bad times without even letting them know...

And in my case...

Love was when he said soft toys are of no use, better buy a pillow or some gadget.. but inspite of that he bought me a new big teddy ..

Love was when he used to say try vodka.. have cigarette but then when I told him that one of my PG-mate was smoking last night.. he started shouting at me and warned me to stay away from that girl.

Love was when he used to call me and we used to talk over nights and hours, just discussing silly things and arguing over topics like Shahrukh Khan and Salman Khan.

Love was when I was totally confused about my career, he was the one who showed me the right way .. suggested me to chase my dreams ... it was he who never said anything.. but was always with me through my good and bad times... whether he was knowing the problem or not...

He never forced me or asked me anything even if he found my phone busy at two in the night. Whenever I felt homesick.. when I was living in a hostel.. he was the one who used to fight with me unnecessarily just to divert my mind and make me smile...

He was always ready with a question "are you happy with this?" in every and whatever things he would do.

We often say love is this and love is that.. we should trust... we should respect... but whatever I experienced was above all... It never came in my mind that he could think of breaking my trust! A blind-faith persuaded in between us. We were totally different. We never discussed about things like giving space to each other or deciding to inform each other about every other situation or incidence.

His faith in us made me feel stronger, he believed in us.

He loved me a lot... No doubt!!

I ruined everything... I shouldn't have written that diary... I shouldn't have made those decisions... I should have been clear with my thoughts and feelings... it was all my mistake...

And he went away...

I wish I could tell him how special he was to me. I wish could let him know how magical it was to be with him, talk to him and listen to him... I wish I could tell him how much I loved him... I wish...

I still, remember the day we met for the first time for fixing of our marriage at my home... like all the arranged marriage customs, my photograph was sent to his place and his to mine. But because of my carelessness, I lost it before I could see it. But my parents had seen the picture and they all liked him a lot. So everybody decided to plan a meet before the final decision of our marriage was taken. I, being a very homely, *agya-kaari,* kind of girl, agreed for this arranged marriage because of two reasons :

(1) I had lost trust in love.

(2) This was the first time that I my parents asked something from me, and I couldn't deny that.

My final year of MJMC was going on. I used to live in Lucknow. I took four days leave from my college and came to Kanpur for this work. I still remember the date – September 15, 2010 which was one of the most memorable days of my life...

# 2

# The First Meeting

With the buzzer of my door-bell, I got my sleep cracked. I was half asleep and half a wakened and could hear the noise of people in my house. Everybody was calling each other for something or some work.. and I could also hear occasional 'Anushree Anushree' by every next person I could hear and especially my mom and my *kaam-waali-bai*. They both were damn worried as it was 9:30 and I was still sleeping despite the fact that today was a big and busy day for me as Vivaan and his family had to visit my home to see me, and to be more precise to check me out whether I was fit enough to get married to their son.

I finally decided to get up when my bhabhi told me that my beautician was waiting for me since one hour.

Ohh!! I jumped over the bed. Today was really a big day for me and I had to look my best today! So, I had booked for a girl from the nearby Lakme parlour to give me a face massage and do my facial.

She did give a face massage and facial to me. It took two hours. Thereafter I was into my wardrobe to search for a perfect dress for that evening. Meanwhile mom entered my room with a brown box in her hands. I was surprised to see it but could make out easily that there was something for me inside it. I opened the box in excitement and to my wonder it was a really pretty red chiffon saree with dark brown embroidered border.

This was really unexpected. I looked at my mom with a blank and astonished expression.. she came near to me, smiled and said, "this is for you!! Wear it today... I am sure you will look like an Indian princess in this attire."

I hugged my mom very tightly. I was almost in tears to receive this unexpected gift from her.

Though I was trying to show as if I was very bold but still I was feeling very hesitant and shy facing everyone at home. I was blushing continuously. The smile couldn't get off my face.

Bhabhi was continuously teasing me 'if this is your situation when you haven't seen him yet, what will happen to you when you will meet him directly'.

Anyhow I managed to communicate with everybody having a control over my emotions, but I decided to get ready by my own with no dark makeup and fixed hairstyle. I preferred looking natural and simple rather than a girl with her face hidden behind a thick layer of makeup.

They were to come at 5 o' clock in the evening.

There were so many things going on in my mind as to – how will I react in front of them, what will I say, what will he ask etc. etc. and above all the bonus question was how does he look? As I hadn't seen his photograph, neither heard his voice...

All I knew was he was born and brought up in Kanpur, he was an investment banker from Mumbai, he had been to foreign countries like America, Europe, etc. for business purpose and have lived there for months, he liked music, he loved to sing and play guitar and not to forget, he had got really killer looks according to my bhabhi.

Oh my god, everything is so difficult. And above all, for the first time I was feeling shy to go in-front of my dad. After every now and then my mother and chachi were instructing me about how I would be behaving in front of them, how would I speak, how would I walk and all that, but I was so nervous as everything was going above my head.

Time that day was running extremely fast. It was 4:30 and I wasn't ready. I rushed to my room to wear saree.

And imagine, in just 10 mins I was perfectly ready. I opened and brushed my hair. Did a very light makeup with nude lip gloss. I wore my favourite *jhumke* and bangles.

And finally, I was ready. It was 5:30 and they were still not here.

Now, this was really not fair... I, along with my whole family and few relatives, were waiting for them and the VIPs were still not here...

But everyone (including me of course) was excited to meet them and the boy perhaps as everybody believed that he was the right guy for me and I should surely get married to him.

Meanwhile we heard a honk. I rushed from that room to another as I had to enter the room only when my mom would call me. This was all pre-planned, about my entry and behaviour. I could hear all the conversation from the next room. I was so excited that I was feeling like running to that room to meet everyone but I had to control.

I was hearing all the conversation and voices of all, but couldn't make out which voice was his. Everybody was talking about the pleasing climate and jams of Kanpur. His mom and my mom were talking about the roads.

Uff, I was feeling as if everything is going down too slow and was feeling like 'uhh come' on call me now, I am ready and I am waiting since a long time.' Yes, I was behaving like a despo that time!!! It was really getting hard to be patient and to wait for someone to call me.

Then I heard my mom asking, 'so, how are you Vivaan?' and for the first time I heard him. He replied – 'I am good aunty, thank you.'

Oh my gosh! His voice was so manly and appealing... by just hearing his voice I could clearly make out that he was a lot like a hunk. Then finally I heard his mom saying so where is Anushree?? And my mom replied – 'oh yes, she is inside preparing stuff to eat, wait I shall call her now. Then mom came in and told me to bring the snacks and coffee.'

My family was quite modern. So, unlike the common scenario where girl enters the room with a tray of tea in her hands, serves everyone with shivering hands and many times like in movies drops down the cup on the groom-to-be's clothes. But I had a maid to serve, I just have to enter like a manager with her and command her to serve people over there. That was quite a good plan and I liked it a lot. So, finally I was going to enter the room and look at Vivaan for the first time. No doubt I was damn nervous and was shivering too. Now I understand why girls shiver and make mistakes and drop down the tray out of their nervousness.

I entered the room, everybody was like – ohh come come. My mom introduced me to his mom- this is Anushree. I gave a smile to aunty i.e. Vivaan's mom and continued to command my maid Vidya to serve coffee.. Everybody was staring at me like anything and I couldn't look at Vivaan. Another reason was I was too shy to look at him. There were six people as guests - Vivaan's mom, dad, his younger brother and sister and Vivaan himself. His sister seemed quite decent. She sat down near me and started throwing questions like what are your hobbies? Who is your favourite actor? And so on.. They cracked jokes as they came to know that Shahrukh was my favourite. And Vivaan used to dislike him. They were cracking jokes like after marriage it seems like we will witness a lot of fights regarding the favourite actor and his movies. We just smiled. Till now half an hour had passed and I hadn't seen him properly.

His dad interrupted the discussion by saying – "now I think we should give Anushree and Vivaan a chance to talk alone and get to know each other" and everybody agreed. Mom ordered my bhabi to take me and Vivaan to the terrace of my home. Vivaan was walking right ahead me, oh my gosh.. he was six ft tall and his personality was truly killer. For the first time I loved following a guy. He and bhabi were talking and I was quietly walking behind them. We reached the terrace. Bhabi left us by wishing us luck just as in the movie *Vivaah*. Rather I should say everything was like in that movie. It was all so perfect and I was perfectly getting nervous. We both were silent until he said – "So, how are you roll number 5?" I was shocked to hear this?

What?? Roll nnumber 5?? I truly had no idea what he was saying. I turned back to him and asked – "Pardon?"

He replied – "I asked how r u roll no 5?"

"Roll no. 5?" – I replied surprisingly.

"Ohh, so you don't remember me? Right?"

"No, sorry?"

"Well, to let you know your highness, we were in the same class till class $6^{th}$. I was roll no. 58 and used to sit at the back..."

"Ohh I am so sorry.. is it so? I'm sorry I really don't remember ?"

"Yeah that's all right, I know.. I was one of the most shabby looking guys of the class and I perfectly understand why would one of the most prettiest girls of the school notice me?"

"Ohh please don't say this? I wasn't..."

"Either you are kidding or you know the truth just u don't wana accept it."

"Why?"

"Yes, you were the most prettiest girls of the school.. the girl in demand.. so, many boys were after you.. everybody wanted to talk to you.. everybody wanted your friendship. Don't you remember?"

"I was really shocked to hear this. This guy was my ex-classmate whom I never noticed?"

He continued, "So, that pretty girl has now turned and grown up into a very beautiful girl I must say..."

All of a sudden all my hestitation was gone. I replied, "Really? Thanks.."

"So, we know each other since childhood?" I tried to crack a joke. We both laughed and then again it was silent. He was just gazing at me and I was blushing. He again initiated, I was thinking that you would still be the same, bubbly, talkative and kiddish but I guess you have become more shy and soft-spoken.

I defended myself by saying "No there is nothing like that.. its just, I require sometime to become free with anyone.. once I am free, I am back to my original avatar." He smiled and said, "So, I am just a stranger to you?"

I replied hesitatingly, "Yeah.. kind of, I really don't remember about you!!"

He laughed on hearing this and said, “Girl, you are really sweet.. ok fine... so, lets start all over again...”

I said “What?”

He said.. “So, you know very well why we are here...”

“Yeah”.

“So, how do you wana start the conversation? Do you wish to know my hobbies or likes or dislikes may be?”

I remained silent.. I was wondering what to ask..

Then I spoke after a gap of few minutes, “I have a question..?”

“Yeeah, sure.. ask?”

“What according to you is important for a relationship to be sustained, is it love, is it trust or is it understanding..”

He without giving any thought to this replied “Of course ‘trust’.”

I smiled and said, ‘Okay...”

He reverted, “And for you?”

I said, “Understanding...”

But surprisingly said, “Why understanding? Why not trust?”

“I have reasons...”, I replied..

“I would like to know them!!” he quoted! “I mean if a person lies to you or hides anything from you then how can you forgive that person and let him go.. I cant forgive a person who had broken my trust..”

"I have my own perception, Mr. Mathur!! According to me, everyone has a genuine reason for hiding anything or lying. In my case, if you or anyone in the world tells and explains me the genuine and real reason for hiding or telling lies, then I would surely understand the problem and forgive him... and if in case that person decided not to tell that thing to me, then I will understand.. that might be a real reason behind that... and I am sure that reason would be genuine,... that kind of understanding I demand from my partner.. and if this kind of understanding prevails in a relationship, then for sure nobody would lie.. nobody would hide anything.."

His expression seemed as if he was spellbound ..he smiled and said, "interesting..."

Cutting the conversation off, I asked "So, did you want to do an arranged marriage or a loved one?"

He looked straight into my eyes and said, "Do you really wana know the answer?"

I diverted my eyes from him and started looking at the sky and said, "Yeah.."

"Well, Anushree this a love marriage from my side..."

I was shocked to hear this... I was frozen. I said, "What????"

"Yes!! And I really thank god for this... I had a huge crush on you, when we were in school... you never talked to me.. although I tried really hard to get noticed by you but you were busy with your stud friends and I just used to look and admire you!! then you suddenly stopped coming to the school.. I thought you left it.. that time there was no means of communication like internet, mobiles etc.. I aske about you from one of your friends who lived nearby your house, she told me that you have left the city.. you along with your parents got shifted to delhi... since then I prayed to god to make me meet you just once, so that I could tell you that there was someone who missed you while you were gone.. then we grew up.. I tried searching you on internet and social networking sites, but found you nowhere.. slowly, I made myself realize that you were gone... forever.. and I was happy living in Mumbai. My parents approached me for marriage.. you know, you were the first girl whom I said yes to meet without knowing anything about you. When I agreed, then my parents told the details about you... don't know why, but my heart wanted to say that it was you only but my mind said don't go on that way.. if she isn't that Anushree Sharma, whom you loved then you will get hurt... I saw your picture but as you are a grown up girl, I couldn't recognize you... finally today I saw you.. and yes, you are the same girl whom I had fallen for when I was a kid... so, I would like to ask you.."

And he suddenly sat on his knees, took my hands and said, "Anushree, will you please marry me and make me the most luckiest guy of this world."

Was all this happening with me in real? I mean I couldn't grasp all this.. few seconds back he was standing and was telling his story.. and now.. he is sitting on his knees and proposing me...

I was silent and wasn't knowing how to react. I was astonished. I gave a thought for a second that if I am really for an arranged marriage then why not him as (1) he is probably the most perfect guy I have ever met and (2) he loves me a lot..

There was so much of truth in his words and love in his heart for me. People say that you should get married to a person who loves you instead to the one whom you love... and Vivaan loved me a lot...

With this thought, I closed my eyes, took a deep breath and replied, "Vivaan ! okay. I will marry you!"

He screamed "Yessssss" with super joy then hugged me tightly and said, "I really love you Anushree. Thanks a lot!!"

He kissed my hands and said, "thank you!! I promise to be with you in your good as well as bad times, in health and sickness, would love you, care for you and respect you. I would never ever leave you... I love you Anushree..."

I was blushing.. I couldn't reply out of my shyness..

He stood up, looking directly into my eyes he said, "You know what? It's a dream come true for me... I am the luckiest person of the world as I am getting married to someone whom I have loved since childhood.. this is what good luck is!!"

I smiled and said... "Shall we go now?"

He said, "Sure after you..."

Oh my goodness, he is such a gentleman.. I wanted to hug him then and there only but naah, have to control my emotions.. we were getting down the stairs silently till my bhabi came and asked, "So, how was everything?"

We both smiled and said "Good" together.. then we three laughed.

Bhabi replied with a notorious smile, "I am expecting to hear a good news.."

We reached the main drawing room. I heard everybody saying, 'ohh here they come'

Vivaan sat near his mom.. and I returned back to my room. Everybody was silent.. I couldn't hear a single word till I heard my brother's voice saying "Ohhh congratulations!!! It is really a good news." And my bhabi and mom came to me.. they asked me what was my decision!!

I wasn't that much sure but on seeing my parent's happiness and Vivaan's love for me I said "Yes" !!! my mom hugged me with super joy. Bhabhi kissed me on my forehead.. and they went back to announce this good news.

Soon, everything was done.. I was being called by Vivaan's parents... Vivaan's mom gifted me a gold-chain and blessed me.. it was pre-planned by dad that if there will be a positive response then we would go out for dinner all together. So, we went out for dinner... me, Vivaan and his siblings sat in one car and other people in rest of two cars.

Vivaan was driving and I was sitting right behind him. He fixed the back mirror on me and was looking on the mirror again and again. His siblings were teasing me but all I could focus on was Vivaan's eyes looking at me again and again... I felt that extraordinary happiness for the first time that day.. I was all red due to shyness...

We had dinner in *Antarang*, which was the most favorite restaurant of my dad...

It was time for a goodbye. Vivaan asked me for my number. We exchanged numbers. We hardly got time to talk alone after everything was fixed. Vivaan's parents suggested that we should get married next month in December as after that Vivaan had to go on a trip to Europe for six months, so he would take me with him there... but everything was going too fast. I wasn't sure I will be able to cope up with the marriage so early..

As by now, it's a love marriage from Vivaan's side but arranged from mine.. and I needed some time to get to know him... I also had to wind up my studies.. they suggested me to drop out the degree in the final semester but I couldn't risk it.. I was interested in doing the job. And it was a masters degree.. I couldn't let go just like that... but I decided not to say anything regarding this at that very moment. I thought to discuss it with Vivaan first..

We came back home at 11:30 p.m.

It was really a busy day. In the morning I was a spinster and right now at night I was an engaged girl. I was about to get married. It was though a very twisted tale kind of a day as I was seriously not expecting this twist about Vivaan knowing me and loving me since childhood...

# 3

# Two Months Later

It was 10:30 at night. I was sitting near my window in my hostel room reading a novel *Aleph* from my favourite author Paulo Coelho.

As it was the month of November, so climate in Lucknow was really very soothing and romantic. It was a silent night. My roommate Nisha wasn't there as she had gone for a night-out with her friends.

Lucky Girl!!

If god would have granted me one wish that time, I would have asked him to replace me with my room-mate.

But without many qualms, I was into my most favorite work i.e. reading a novel.

While *Aleph* was getting much more interesting, suddenly my mobile beeped. It was a chat message on *whatsapp* by V*ivaan*.

It was, "Hey there?"

I replied, "What?"

Vivaan, "Madam, are you free tomorrow?"

I, "Why? got some work?"

Vivaan, "I am coming to Lucknow."

I, "Really?"

Now Instead of replying for this message, he called me up!

I picked up the call and said, "Vivaan are you seriously coming tomorrow or you are just kidding???"

He laughed and said, "Nooo why would I be kidding??? I not a kid like you!!!"

"Shut-up you!! Answer me??? You *sach mein* coming to Lucknow???"

He said, "Yepp!! I am..."

It was quite unbelievable that he suddenly made a program of visiting Lucknow that too in the month of November. I was really excited to hear this as after we got our marriage fixed in September, this was the first time when we were going to meet...

Till now, after a span of two months of a long distance relationship, I had started falling for Vivaan in real. His way of talks, this accent, his humour, his likes and dislikes ; all were over me ... I used to discuss about him every now and then with my best friends. He was a perfect guy for me... we used to have long day chats and over-night phone calls... I was getting addicted to him and by that time, I had also realized that I had fallen for him... and my decision of accepting his proposal for marriage was not at all wrong...

I was finally happy...

We had a long conversation, he told me about his program for visiting Lucknow. Then he shall leave for Delhi that night only. It is because, of his flight schedule that he had to plan a break journey from Mumbai to Lucknow then from Lucknow to Delhi. But he did not reveal the next day's programme!

It was the day when *Harry Potter and the Half Blood* Prince was going to be released and one of the most common thing in between us which made us more compatible was that we both loved *Harry Potter* series. It is so good that we have atleast this 'Harry Potter love' common in ourselves, because nothing in the world was common in us except this.. if I liked love stories, then he loved to read and watch crime fiction. I loved Indian music and he loved jazz. I loved burger and he loved samosa.. But when it comes to Harry Potter... we both loved it So, It was default by that we would be going to watch that movie. If he wouldn't have planned for it then obviously I had planned so...

The next morning I woke up at 7:30 with Nisha's voice shouting "Anushree - Anushree" knocking at the door very loudly!

Yeek!! I hate getting up so early. Especially when my sleep is interrupted with these sort of unwanted voices. I got up... opened the door and crash landed again on my bed.

When I was just about to fall-asleep, my phone rang. It was Vivaan... so early again!!

In a very sleepy voice I received his call and said, "Hewllo! Uuhhh!!"

Him, "You still sleeping? Get up and get ready I'll be there by 11."

I replied, "Why should I get ready now? Its so early!"

He said, "Madam, wake up!! I am leaving for Lucknow in few minutes."

Me, "Its more than 3 hours. I'll get up at 10:30 and would get ready by 11."

Him, "No!! You girls take a lot of time to get ready. I order you. Get up now!!"

Me, "Okay okay ! Just five minutes more."

Him, "Okay. But only five minutes!!"

Me, "Hmmm!"

Him, "Listen, boarding is done. I am in flight so I have to switch off my phone now. So, get up, and bye!!"

Me, "Hey listen?"

Him, "What? Speak fast? That steward is staring at me as if I am a terrorist!"

Me, "Happy Journey."

With his reply, "Thank you sooooo much, now bye," he disconnected the phone call.

I again did a crash landing on my bed and went off to sleep. I didn't come to know when I went off to sleep so deeply. With a phone ring I got up. It was mumma's call. My mumma!

I received it and again spoke in the same sleepy tone without opening my eyes properly. I greeted mumma with a very good-morning as always.

"Anushree, its 11:30.. get up", Mom said and on hearing this jumped off from my bed. She also told that Vivaan was already there in Lucknow. He was trying to call me but I wasn't picking up his call.

Damn!! So He called up mumma and told her to wake me up!

Well... after this conversation with my mom, I called back Vivaan.

Instead of hello, he said, "Good morning madam!" in a very cheesy tone.

I replied, "Where are you??"

He uttered, "Aaa listen!!"

And before listening to anything I said, "See I am really very sorry! Just give me five minutes and I will be ready."

Vivaan said, "Listen, come to your window!!" he sounded as if he was smiling and excited too. But I was confused on hearing this.

I replied, "What??"

Vivaan, "Yeah! come!!"

"Where?????", I confirmed

"To your window madam!!!", said he.

I rushed to the window, opened it up. with the flash of sunlight direct into my eyes, I went blind for some seconds. After gaining back my vision, I tried to look for him. But he was no-where. I thought he might be joking. But still I was trying to figure him out as where he was!!

I asked him, "What is happening? Are you really here..??" and as I was saying this, From the corner of the window I saw him with a group of kids who surrounded him.

I shouted, "Hey" from my window and tried to give a wave to him from my window but as my window's railing was just similar to the railing of a jail, I was unable to!

Now this was quite a weird behaviour but in excitement I lose all my powers to think like a gentle –lady and turn out into a kid!!

I disconnected the phone call and went running downstairs to meet him in my sleeping-midi dress; without brushing my hair properly and above all, with my chappals on.

The moment I reached near him, all kids came running towards me with hands at their back as if they were hiding something. I wondered what was happening!!

I looked at Vivaan and asked "What" by nodding my head with raised eye-brows.

He smiled and said "for you...!!!"

I replied, "What???"

He shouted, "kiiiiidddsssss????"

And all kids started shouting "Didiiiiiii" and then each one of them presented me with a Red and Orange Gerbera.

It was breathtaking and a pleasure surprise for me.

Oh my Goodness!! Gerberas were my favorite flowers. I loved them.

But flowers and Mr. Vivaan Mathur?

Now this was really weird!! When I used to say flowers are the most wonderful gift then he used to say they are nothing but wastage of money, gift something useful instead. And now he gifted me flowers that too my favourites... Not bad Mr. Vivaan!! Not Bad!!

I took all the flowers from all the kids and those kids ran away instantly.

I went near Vivaan.

I was so happy to see him that I couldn't control myself. I hugged him on the road and screamed "thank-you" loudly near his ears.

He replied clearing his ears with his finger, "Thank you??? For what???"

He no doubt was the most good looking guy I have ever met. He looked awesome in every gesture of his, even when he was clearing his ears with fingers.

Awww, this was my Vivaan, every girl felt jealous on seeing me and Vivaan together and I loved that.

I said showing him the flowers, "For these...!! They are sooooo lovely..!! thank you... really!!!"

"Okay okay! You are most welcome. Now go and get ready or else, we will miss our show!!", said he making himself seated on the balcony of a general merchants shop in front of my hostel.

I with excitement asked him, "Are we going to Harry Potter?"

"Do you have any doubt?" he replied with a smile.

I said, "Just give me ten mins. And I'll be here again" running back towards my hostel's entrance door.

I reached my room. Kept all the flowers on my study desk in a water-jug!! I was taking out my clothes from the wardrobe in a hurry, meanwhile my room mate Nisha came out of the washroom.

She held me from my waist and asked, "What happened? You going to college??"

I said removing her hands from my waist, "No!! I am bunking today!!"

"Then where are you going??" she inquired.

"Its Vivaan here!" I replied and returned back to finalize the dress for myself.

Nisha asked surprisingly, "Who Vivaan??"

I replied, "Ahhh my fiancée stupid!! I have told you about him many a times are you still in a hangover??? Don't you remember? Silly...!!! Being my roomie, you don't even remember my fiancee's name!!"

Yes, this was the kind of relation we room-mates used to share. We never ever interfered in each other's personal life and neither we took any interest... the only thing we loved doing together was Shopping!! Yeah, we loved shopping and went shopping every weekend... and sometimes on weekdays too.. also there was a ritual that we have to go for shopping during exams!! Weird it may sound though, but it's the truth!! We were true shopaholics!! And if coming back to our personal lives, I should confess that I didn't even know the name of her boyfriend...

Finally after wondering for few seconds, she said, "Oh yeah!! So he is here? For what?"

I was busy in digging out my wardrobe. I exclaimed, "White kurti!! Yes!!"

She asked me again giving a puzzled expression, "*Hain???* He is here for a white kurti?"

"Oh no no! white kurti –I'll be wearing! He is on for a conference in Delhi. He had a break journey via Lucknow and has a flight to Delhi tonite, that is why he is here. He is standing downstairs and we are already late just because of me!! and you istead of helping me out to finalize my dress, are asking so many questions. Listen up, I am really in a rush right now. So, Bye–bye!!"

"Oh-kay ! go-on, by the way really beautiful flowers!!" she said pointing towards the flowers.

"Don't touch them!!" I shouted rushing towards the washroom.

I took a bath within five minutes dressed myself up in the pair of a basic blue jeans and a short white kurti.

Picked up my side-bag and ran downstairs.

Vivaan was waiting for me there only where I left him..

It was already 12:15 by then and we had to catch up for the movie at one.

We rushed to the nearby taxi-stand. Hired a taxi for the Phoenix Mall where Harry Potter and the Half Blood Prince was being shown.

Either it was actually something different or it was the impact of our meeting for the first time that we were sitting silently inside the taxi. We were actually not getting any topic to start up with. We used to have long phone call chats after we got committed, which seemed to be never ending. But now... we were sitting quietly!!

Still like a casual conversation starter dialogues I asked him, "So ? how was your journey?"

He replied, "Good!!"

Geez! What was happening ? again it was silence between us. I was trying to remember any of our common interest topics but my mind went blank all the time. My wet and open hair were annoying me so I was trying to tie them up.

But suddenly Vivaan interrupted me and said, "Leave them as they suit you a lot. You are really looking beautiful!"

For the first time Vivaan appreciated me sitting next to me!! I wanted someone to come and hide me.. I was blushing like anything.. shyness was its heights.

Then I thought, "Come on Anu darling, he is Vivaan – your would be hubby!! ! Blushing is really not required. Control yourself!!"

In a very kiddish tone I replied "Really? thank you sooooo much!" so that he couldn't notice my blushing face or else he might think something fishy. And so on demand, I left my hair as they were.

We reached the Mall, it was already 12:55. He rushed to buy tickets and me towards the *nachos* stall. But as the food counter was also crowded, I returned back near the ticket counter and decided to wait for Vivaan there only.

"Oh my Geez!! It's so much crowd here. I wonder there are so many Potter fans like us." I murmured this to myself. It seemed next to impossible to get the tickets but luckily we got them. After buying tickets, Vivaan went to buy Pepsi, popcorn and nachos off-course, to munch in between the movie.

Soon we were seated.

Watching Harry Potter may it be any part of it, is like a treat to the eyes. I was enjoying each and every moment of the movie. There was a scene in it when Ron asks Harry, "Don't you think Hermoine is really good?"

Harry replies, "Ahh never thought off!"

Ron says, "Still... say something at least?"

Harry says, "Yeah, umm her skin is good."

Everybody in the theatre laughed at the dialogues of Harry and so did I, but Vivaan leaned towards me and said, "Even you have a very good skin!"

I was like "What??" but I said, "Thanks!! really!!"

After this incident, my mind couldn't focus on the movie. What all was going inside my mind was the moments of appreciation which Vivaan gave to me. The way he gifted me the flowers, the chocolate, appreciated my hair and now skin! He wasn't focusing on the movie. I was feeling a new vibe in between us or may be the vibe was old only I didn't realize about it.

After the movie we went to a Chinese restaurant for lunch. For that day, I was the guide so after lunch, we went to my favorite place in Lucknow. It was the first time when Vivaan was about to see the *marine-drive* in Lucknow. Previously, Whenever I use to tell him about my outing with friends at Marine Drive he use to tease me by saying, "Say local Marine Drive rather! As actually MD is in Mumbai. People give names to the places, according to their fantasies. Now they can't go to the original marine drive so they named some local spot as MD!!"

I always got annoyed by this argument of his and always -let him speak!! one day, when I would take him to Marine Drive of Lucknow then I would ask his views about it.

It was 6:15 when we reached there. He was truly mesmerized watching that view through the Marine Drive, it started drizzling and with all the glowing lamp-shades, the view really became like a scenic landscape.

We walked all around here and there, down the streets just looking at each other and smiling. We trespassed the boundary to reach the other lane. He held me through my waist while jumping over the boundary wall. I was feeling very weird as it was his first touch. Although it may sound like a script of 1960's movie but we actually never even had shook hands before. This was the second time when he touched me... first time was when he proposed me on my terrace, the day we got committed.

Today in the morning was the first hug of ours, which I gave him when he presented me the flowers and now this one...

There came a moment when we were about to cross the road. Traffic was really high at that time. We were just about to cross the road suddenly he got a phone call from one of his colleagues. As I was, actually I am really phobic of crossing the roads alone I thought for a while to hold his hands by myself but then thought what he would wonder if I held his hands. He was busy talking on phone. I was walking a step behind him. On reaching the verge of the road, he by himself offered me his hands to hold. I was surprised with joy as this was really unexpected. I held his hands tightly and we crossed the road. For the first time then, I felt that I am here in safe hands and nothing can go wrong now.

We ate *pani-poories*, he also bought me balloons when I insisted.

How cute he is..!!

He took me for shopping too in-spite of he being a shopping-allergic person. After trying so many dresses, he finally chose, finalized and bought a black midi-dress for me and with that, our shopping was done!!

I was noticing one thing, that Vivaan was repeating one thing again and again 'Anushree, you are the same as you were when we were kids... you are totally full of life, you love to enjoy each and every moment and above all I am that first lucky guy in your life whom you love..."

Although it was true, and I have never been in a relationship... or may be I was... but I don't think that was a relationship... I was not certain as to what was that in my past but whatever it was... I never wanted to recall it... but still it was something which Vivaan was unaware of... something which was unknown to Vivaan... something a guy should know about the girl whom he is getting married to and for the first time, I felt that I should have discussed things about my past life with him, and then we should have taken the decision to get married...

It was already 8'o clock and he had a flight at 9:30. He insisted me to come to the airport with him and told me that a friend of his would drop me home by car. He called his friend, Rishu who came with a car and took us to the airport.

In Lucknow airport, visitors are not allowed to go inside the airport so we were standing outside the airport and talking. It was 9'o clock.

Again initiating as the conversation starter, I said, "Day was fun! Right?"

He replied, "Yeah, but one thing is still left!"

I questioned, "What?"

He sat on his knees in front of the crowd, held my left hand's palm and took out a diamond ring. He was again on his knees, and this time with a diamond ring.

I was speechless...

He took my hands and made me wear that ring and said, "This beautiful ring for the most beautiful girl in the whole world.."

I went blank at that moment. I was not knowing what to say or react. I have seen these kind of scenes in the movies but this was actually happening to me in reality. I left his hands and pinched myself to make sure that I wasn't dreaming. And to my wonders, I wasn't!!

I was speechless and was trying to make him stand up so that all those people who were staring at us like anything would get back to their work.

He insisted, "Ain't you happy?"

In the dilemma, I replied, "No! I mean what? I don't know! It is so expensive".

"Are you kidding aAree??", Vivaan replied in an annoying tone.

"See, to be very frank I don't think it is right to accept this expensive gift right now.." I said while taking off the ring from my finger. He tried to stop me but I continued, "See, next month in December we are getting officially engaged.. I would feel really happy if you gift me this ring then and make me wear it in-front of all the people."

He was sad but I couldn't help it... this was correct... I wasn't like other girls who love to take expensive gifts from their boyfriends or fiancées ... I never had accepted this much of expensive gift... I did what my heart said...

"See Anushree, this is my point.. I want us to get married next month so that I can take you with me to Europe!!", Vivaan seemed impatient.

But I was shocked and getting married next month was just not possible..

I asked Vivaan to go right now as he was getting late and told him that we would talk on this matter later on phone. I also told him not to discus anything regarding this with family...

He hugged me and said "Okay, whatever makes you happy!!"

I smiled "Thanks Vivaan,,,"

He again hugged me and said, "I should be going now... although I wish I could stay here with you forever... but Anushree, I will come and take you with me forever..."

I smiled and said, "I will wait for you Vivaan..."

I pushed him towards the airport entrance and said, "Now go!"

He smiled, picked up his luggage, hugged his friend and started moving towards the entrance.

I shouted, "Hey???"

He turned back and said, "What??"

I replied, "Happy Journey!!!!"

With his killer smile, he replied, "Thanks" and went inside the airport...

# 4

# What to Do?

It was 10 p.m. when I reached my hostel.

As my hostel is not a college hostel actually but an independent girl's hostel near my campus, the in-charge is the owner of the hostel and we call her Digi Aunty. Digi aunty is very particular about her rules and regulations and she had strictly warned all girls to reach the hostel by 9.

As it was already 10, I was really scared to enter the hostel as Digi aunty would be ready with mobile phone in her hands to make a call at my home and tell my family that I came to the hostel at 10!!! But luckily, Digi aunty with her family had gone out for a party and so I entered the hostel very easily.

Nisha was waiting for me for dinner. We always used to have dinner together. As I entered my room, she starting shooting questions at me.

Oh geez!! Why This girl is always full of questions in her mouth-bag?

"Where were you whole day? Why are you so late? you are never late? Its 10? Is all fine? You should have informed me? I was worried!! And I was waiting for you for dinner? And where is your mobile? It was switched-off, why so? I was so hungry!"

Oh My God!!!!

As I was a bit out of my mind, I silently lay down on my bed without answering to any of her questions.

She came near me and asked, "Hey!! are you alright?"

I nodded my head to reply yes.

She again said, "You don't look so??? What's the matter??"

I looked at her and said, "I am sorry. Phone's battery got discharged. I was with Vivaan whole day. Right now I am coming back from the airport. Went to see him off with his friend."

Nisha said, "Madam You don't look normal? Are you upset or something?"

I replied, "Go and have dinner first. We'll talk later on."

"Did you have your dinner?" –she inquired.

"Yeah! Now go."

She went away and I was just lying down on my bed with thoughts wandering on my mind.

I was all lost as to what all happened. What should I do? I cannot get married next month. But I don't want to hurt Vivaan too. I wasn't getting anything.

Nisha, after having her dinner again came to me and asked, "Now tell whats wrong with you?"

I replied, "Vivaan wanted us to get married next month".

"And????" inquired Nisha.

"And I don't know what to do!!"-I was really out of my mind.

"Gosh girl, get married... it is so exciting!! It's a time to celebrate... idiot!!"-Nisha said while she caught hold of my hand.

I was sad. I looked into her eyes and said, "It's not about celebrations mate! I am just not..."

"Just not... what?????" –She retaliated.

"I am just not ready..."

She asked – "not ready for what?"

"For marriage you silly!!"-things were really getting over my nerves.

"Spit-out whatevér is going on in your mind."Nisha said calming me down.

I remained silent. Actually I wasn't getting what to explain to her. What was the reason? Why I wasn't ready... it was for sure that they means Vivaan's family and him of course would not ruin my studies and make me drop in between... and if it was about going to Europe for six months then I could easily get off from college as it was my training semester and I had to go for training of six months.. Everything at college can be handled easily... but then..

The reason was something else... may be in the corner of my heart, I wanted to tell each and everything about my past life to Vivaan... but I was scared... to loose him... and if I was in Vivaan's place, I would have done the same!!!

But... having a look at my past records, every now and then, I had to face certain problems caused by people in my life!! Either by rumors or by themselves directly entering my life... and if after marriage, Vivaan would hear certain things about me by any other sources, then it would surely be difficult to handle him... as Vivaan was really a short-tempered guy... and I was really scared of his anger!!!

I was still silent and wondering what to do!!

She again insisted, "I promise I wont tell it to anyone. Trust me!!"

I took Nisha to the terrace. Terrace was the only place in my hostel where we got blessed with privacy and could talk our hearts out.

I sat down on the floor and started with my part of the story- "Vivaan is a guy of dignity and principles which he would never think of compromising with. Soon Vivaan will leave for Europe for his company's onsite project, but before that he wants us to get married so that he can take me with him to Europe for few months...

Vivaan and I were in the same class till sixth as I have told you before but then I had to leave the school as my father was being transferred to Delhi, so me and my family got shifted there. After that we met each other when the meeting was arranged by our parents for our marriage. There Vivaan re-introduced himself and also told me that he had loved me since childhood but as I left the school when we were kids," I continued, 'and as I wasn't friends with Vivaan during school, he never expressed anything to me, although he told me that he tried a lot during school to talk to me and share friendship with me but I never responded to him... he had a secret crush on me since then!! So, finally that day when we met, he proposed to me and expressed all his feelings and whatever he had gone through during these years to me.'

"Hey, so what is the matter?" Nisha interrupted in between, 'I mean, All is set. You both know each other since childhood. He is well settled with a good job. Family background is good, he loves you a lot and above all this marriage is arranged by your parents. Now where the hell does the complication lie?"

"No!" I said, "He hardly knows me, about my past life. We were in different schools after sixth, then different colleges and now different cities. What all happened in my life in between is not known to him. He is a guy who can bear anything on the earth except a lie!"

"Did you lie to him on anything?" asked Nisha.

I, "No ! I never did. Actually we never had a talk about what was going in our personal lives? Or what all we have gone through ? How had the day been and all? So, I never got a chance to discuss anything regarding all that with him."

Nisha, "So tell him now?"

I, "So I can't. Now he would think that I kept all that hidden from him and I never let him know about all that knowingly. He would not trust me."

Nisha, "But he is your would behusband. He has a right to know everything about your life. May it be your past, present or future."

I – "I will tell him everything. All I want is time. I do not want to get married so soon. I just want him to fall in love with me more deeply and have utmost trust in me so that when I tell him about my past life, he should not get angry and think that I willingly kept everything hidden from him."

Nisha – "Tell him that you don't want to get married so early. Tell him that you are ready for the engagement but not for the marriage... I am sure, he would understand."

I – "Hmm yeah! I will... lets see what happens..."

Meanwhile my phone started ringing!

It was Tanshika, my sister, neighbour cum best friend.

She was the only one who knew each and everything about me and my past life.

I in a hurry picked up her call and said, "Tanshi I was really about to call you right now."

She replied, "Congratulations Anu! I am so happy for you."

I, "How did you come to know?"

Tanshi, "Off-course Vivaan, rather I should say *jiju* told me."

I, "So you knew about this plan of his?"

Tanshi, "Of course dear. I knew the whole scene. Yesterday-night Vivaan called me up and told me each and everything. Gosh ! he was really damn scared. I am so happy that you said yes to him. He really loves you a lot."

I, "Tanshi, listen to me first. Even I know he loves me, family agreed for us and all the things for heaven's sake. But I can't get married so soon!! You know what all I have faced after changing the school and college. If he by any chance comes to know all that after our engagement or marriage, then he would surely leave me. And yes, its truth that I don't want to loose him. Because now I love him too. And I can't pretend to be what I am not and what he thinks

I was and I am... I don't want to hurt him. And also I don't want him to think of me as a liar..."

Tanshi, "What is happening to you Anu? Everything is set here. You are getting a life partner who has loved you since he was just 3 or 4 years of age and you are thinking of all that past and negative things happened in your life? For God's sake forget all that and try to begin a new life with him."

I, "I can't. I mean, even I want to forget all those things happened but I am unable to. Things are unfinished. My questions are still unanswered. I am scared Tanshi. I feel like something is stuck inside me from the past because of which I am unable to let it all go."

Tanshi, "It may be because Vivaan doesn't knows all this and you are scared what will happen if he comes to know all of a sudden?"

I – "I don't know. May be you are right. Even my room-mate is suggesting the same thing".

Tanshi, "So now??"

I – "She is forcing me to tell each and everything about myself to him."

Tanshi – "Yes, you should even I was about to say the same thing."

I – "Tanshi..."

– "What ????"

I – "But how can I tell him? Its just not possible to narrate him the whole journey of ten years on phone-call and to be very frank, even I don't have guts to tell him all that directly. After all he trusts me a lot."

Tanshi – "I have an idea!!"

I – "What?"

Tanshi – "See, first you call your mom and tell her that you don't want to get married next month. Then next month he is coming to Kanpur for a week, right?"

I, "Right!"

Tanshi –"You write all the things in a diary, which you want to tell him. Write your heart out. Even whatever you feel about him, jot that down too. And then give that diary to him and tell him to read when you are gone."

I – "Will this work?"

Tanshi – "Yeah! Of-course. Go for it. You have a month to write. It'll be sufficient for you to write the story of your past life."

And with this, we ended our conversation.

I discussed all the matter with two more of my friends and they agreed too.

Next day, I called my mother followed by Vivaan and told them very frankly that I am not willing to get married next month. I told them the reason that I have studies to do and focus on my career and surely after marriage I would not be able to do all this...

And to my surprise, they both agreed very simply with me.

I wonder Sometimes it's the complication which just lies in our minds. I was thinking that I had to answer many questions to them and had to try hard to convince them about my decision. But it all went in a very simple way.

Soon I began to write up my story...

I started it from the year 1999, the year when I left all and went to Delhi with my family...

# 5

# December is Here

Finally it was the month of December. I finished writing my story. It covered almost a whole diary. My goodness, I wondered was my story so long that it covered a whole three hundred page diary?

Well, It was a day before when Vivaan was about to come to Kanpur. Actually there are no direct flights to Kanpur from Mumbai, so he was to reach Amausi airport situated at the outskirts of Lucknow and then move to Kanpur via road.

One of his friends Kartik, who was a colleague of mine called me up at night, and we decided to give a surprise to Vivaan by going and receiving him from the airport. All was set. The only thing left was rising of the sun bringing a new dawn with himself.

Third December; Monday morning, 7 o' clock – the day when I had to face Vivaan after a span of a month. This span of a month was quite interesting...

By now, we had started behaving like the typical committed couple. He used to call me up every morning as soon as he got up, and we talked every night before sleeping.

While he was at work and I in college, we continued chatting on *whatsapp messenger*. It had become like a habit... or may be we were addicted to each other by now!!

But in any case, talking on phone was much easier than facing directly... and today was the day!! I don't know whether I was the only one who is so much shy of her fiancée or all girls on earth behave in this way only.. but whatever it may be, I was too shy to face him!!

Still, it was half an hour for his flight to land and I, along with two friends were already there. Every minute I was gazing at my watch to check out the time. This was the first time when I was feeling nervous and excited along with a feeling of shyness to face Vivaan for the first time. I never felt that before. I was wondering about what would be his reaction after looking at me. Would he run towards me and hug me tightly or it would be a formal hi-hello when people usually meet and greet. I wasn't getting how I would be reacting when I would see him.

With all this dilemma, half hour passed and my phone rang. It was Vivaan.

I picked up and spoke in a very nervous tone – "Hello?"

Vivaan – "Anu my Jaanu, I've reached Amausi airport."

I replied – "That's really nice. Anybody coming to receive you?"

Vivaan – "Just a sec! let me collect my baggage."

I – "Yeah sure!"

I was blushing on the phone and my face was shining as if 100 watt bulbs are being exposed to it.

Vivaan again – "Yeah u there?"

I – "Yeah?"

Vivaan – "So, what were you saying?"

'Well, I was asking did anybody come to receive you?' I was trying to engage him in talking till he comes out and sees me standing at the door to welcome him.

'I don't know. I'm so stupid. I should have called home to seek information regarding this and I called you to chit chat.' Vivaan giggled loudly.

'But no worries, I'll hire a taxi from here.' He continued.

I replied ok and saw Vivaan coming out of the door. Oh my Gosh ! He was looking so handsome for the first time in black t-shirt and dark blue denims with shades on him.

I wonder Vivaan should try modeling as he was in Mumbai and he looked awesome and would easily get assignments on modeling!!

But I never suggested as firstly he was least interested and secondly, life of these models is just not my types. I mean I can't imagine Vivaan being with and posing with other girls in sexy outfits for the photo-shoots!! And if I sound possessive right now, then I was, am and will be possessive for him always...

I was totally spellbound and remained quiet.

Call was on, Vivaan said –'There na??'

"Ohh yes!! I am here" I replied coming back to my senses.

"Dear, are you somewhere outside? There's so much of noise coming from the back." Inquired Vivaan.

I replied, "yes!"

Vivaan shot another question on me, "Where? You didn't tell me that you had plans for today."

"Yeah. It was sudden plan actually."

"Ok, so where are you?" asked Vivaan.

By now, he was standing right in-front of me and was looking here and there.

"Just in front of you".

On hearing this Vivaan started looking here and there.

As he saw me, he dropped all his baggage and also his phone.

Oh my God! I screamed and ran towards him to pick his luggage and of-course his phone too. Phones are of much importance these days I must say. He shouldn't have dropped that. But look at him, he was standing like a statue with a big smile gazing towards me was if he is not believing that I was there to receive him.

I and his friends went near him. I picked up his phone and said, "Are you nuts? You dropped your Iphone?"

Vivaan touched my cheeks with one finger and said, "Are you really here Anu?"

I smiled and looked into his eyes and said, "Yes! see..." and I offered my hands towards him to make him believe that I was actually standing infront of him.

He held my hands, then kissed my palms and said, "I really missed you a lot. Thanks a lot for coming."

With the honk of the car horn, Ritesh interrupted us and shouted sitting from the car, "Oh hello? Can you guys continue your romantic chit-chat in the car? We have to reach Kanpur on time, especially you madam Anu?"

"Oh yes! I forgot!! Mom has allowed just for four hours. I have to be there at home by 12!" I replied while moving towards the car.

Me and Vivaan were sitting at the back seat and Kartik -Ritesh in front.

It was too cold as it was the month of December. But no doubt the view was awesome. Especially if you are with the one you love, it was the perfect view of the green fields plus the romantic songs which were being played in the car. It was Mr. Ritesh's choice to play bollywood romantic songs just to tease us and also for the reason that Vivaan and I loved bollywood songs. He started with the song "*Pehla pehla pyar hai*" of *Hum Aapke Hai Haun* followed by several songs like "*pehla nasha*" "*Tum mile*" "*Dil ibadat kar raha hai*" "*Soniyo mera saath do*" "*khuda jaane*" and so on...

Vivaan was sitting and smiling and I was blushing like anything. It seemed like Vivaan was trying to find out a chance to hold my hands. So, I made it easy for him by keeping my left hand in between us just as if I was taking my hand's rest to sit.

And Bingo! he kept his hand on my hands. Soon our fingers were clutched into each others. This was for the first time happening with me and Vivaan that Vivaan was holding my hands with this much of affection. That moment I felt 'Yes... I am in love now' !!!

It was simply unbelievable for me that Vivaan was so romantic in nature.

I was totally lost in all these thoughts of mine and suddenly I felt the warmth of his breath near my ears. It was the time that my heartbeats were running so fast that I could hear them clearly. I tried to look at him. He was so close. Just about two inches far from my face. He came near my lips. I closed my eyes with nervousness and also for the reason to experience world's best feeling for the first time. Two seconds later, He kissed me but on my forehead and said, "I really love you Anushree".

I opened my eyes which were full of tears. These were the tears of joy and happiness. That very moment I decided that I would not give that diary to him in which I have written about my past life. I hugged him very tightly and so did he.

With the Notorious "Ahem Ahem" of Kartik, we were interrupted.

Kartik with a tricky raised eye-brow expression looked at us and said, "Control guys, control!!"

And those three guys in the car laughed out loudly and I with embarrassment kept my head down for ten minutes.

Time passed so soon there in the car with him and his friends that we felt like some moments ago we met and now we have reached Kanpur.

I wish we would have continued that journey ... but it was time to go. They dropped me to my home. Vivaan met my mom just like a typical son in law by touching her feat and greeting her.

Soon they went off and again. We were online on *whatsapp messenger* to talk with each other.

He was here for four days only. Wednesday we had our engagement and Friday night it was his flight back to Mumbai.

As it was all clear in my mind that I was not going to give him my diary... as everything was so perfect and I didn't want to ruin these moments of happiness by giving him my diary and making him upset.

Wednesday was our engagement day!!

**The Engagement**

I got up hearing faint voices and people chattering over various issues, children playing around with their mothers after them. It was my engagement day. Far off relatives had started coming in right from the morning and in no time our house would no longer be a dwelling of five but home to around fifty people. The elderly were busy managing the responsibilities given to them to make sure no part of the ritual gets affected; the children were busy planning for various games and cuisines they were going to enjoy. The rest of the party would be joining us in the banquet hall, the Ved. This also marks the official beginning of the Hindu ritualistic wedding ceremony which could last a month.

Greeted with smiles on faces, cousins teasing with all sorts of jokes, taking elders' blessings I settled among my cousins and started discussing about the day's proceedings. They had got everything planned from taking me to the beauty parlor and then to the venue. On hearing out their mischievious plans for the eve, I was sure Vivaan would be in for surprises today.

It was by noon I had to make it to the parlour with Asha, my cousin, who would be escorting me to the parlour.

Vivaan doesn't like me to put much of a makeup but today it couldn't be avoided as people would be watching us so we had to look perfect, if it takes anything. After four long hours of foundation, toning, mascara and all sorts of foreign products which these parlours use to fetch maximum cash out of you and completely make you up for an entire evening or a day so, it was time for me to leave for the venue. Vivaan's side was expected to be there in about two hours.

It was 5:30 pm. Asha and I reached the venue shortly. It was fully decorated with lights and garlands and looked no less than a perfect abode of angels. With a magenta saree embroidered with lace and Resham work in blue which added a sign of *desi* beauty to the attire and the jewellery and necklace complemented the tone of the saree. The wedding bangles were no less attractive. My father could not resist himself as soon as he saw me and kissed me on my forehead and gave blessings for life. My aunts and uncles made me realize how much similar my mom was looking when she got married. Nothing could be more beautiful than this moment. I wanted to enjoy every moment of the eve today.

Soon I was taken upstairs to the hotel room where I had to wait until Vivaan's family arrived. He was in the city for a couple of days only so they had to manage everything pretty fast. The two families worked in co-ordination to make everything properly managed for the eve. I was lot more excited than being nervous. After all, it has been a wait for years for this day to come. While my cousins took pictures with me in turns, I recalled all that had happened until now and how Vivaan and I ended up making it to this day. I was happy. I was content.

There was a knock on the door and to my surprise, my very beloved cousin; Harsh was standing with lots of chocolates in his hand. He had been making excuses to me that he won't be able to attend the engagement as he was occupied with lots of work and that his manager was not allowing him leaves. But all of those reasons were made up by him by this surprise visit. I was overwhelmed and hugged him. The level of joy just reached enormous heights and even others were also excited to see him.

Soon Vivaan and family had arrived at the venue. All my cousins rushed to see him. I was left with one of my aunts. Vivaan and his parents were the first to come, followed by their relatives. As I was described later, my brothers welcomed them with the bouquets and the two sides greeted each other. Vivaan was dressed in white cotton shirt and a straight fit black trouser with derby shoes which portrayed his simplicity. My aunts were impressed by the way he carried himself all along the party and his way of getting accustomed to people revealed his down to earth nature. While the elderly from the two families were getting familiar to each other and heads of the family were blessing the youngsters, Vivaan and family were escorted towards the *puja-sthal* where all rituals would be performed.

The first of all proceedings is the *Bariksha* which marks the commencement of the wedding alliance. *Bariksha* is supposed to be more of a male-centric ritual where the bride-to-be's brother offers gifts to the groom-would-be. My brother, Nikhil, was too excited for this as he now considered himself to be of high importance in participating in the Tilak ceremony. The gifts include clothes, sweets and fruits and other items for the groom along with cash. After the *Bariksha* ceremony, it was time for the *Tilak* ceremony wherein the bride-to-be's family offers gifts and sweets to the groom-to-be's family members to accept it as a token gesture of confirmation of relationship of the two families.

After completion of both the rituals, it was time for '*God Bharai Rasam*' or the *Baby Shower Ritual*. Having all the three under a common roof and on the same day is a general trend these days. Due to such busy lives professionally, it is not possible for everyone to come to every event held over a period of month on different days. Instead, to pace with the current generation, people tend to celebrate them together for everyone's ease.

Everyone at the hall entrance was waiting to get the first glimpse of me as if I was some diva. Just the moment when I was about to enter the hall, we were asked to stop as there was some confusion in Vivaan's family over some matter unknown to me. Surprised by this sudden halt, one of my cousin informed me that Vivaan's family had been making some last moment arrangements before I could step in and they wanted to make sure everything is at its place before the ritual begins.

While I was standing there being the center of attraction to many, some of my family members, especially the youngsters were busy getting a photograph with me and everyone wanted to have one. Suddenly, to my amazement, my mother-in-law came in to see me and gave me heartfelt blessings. It was a perfect moment of many to watch me and my mother-in-law having our little formal chat and I, being the bride-to-be behaved in the manner which every Indian girl would before her mother-in-law. My close college friends and some of my office colleagues congratulated me. I was also missing my bestie, Tanshika, who told me that she won't be able to make it to the ceremony as she had some very important and unavoidable meeting at her office at this time. I was a bit off with her too for not being there with me on my special day. Soon it was a green signal for me to step into the hall.

While I walked down the red carpet slowly, my cousins and family members smiled at each other and my younger cousin beside me took full pride in walking alongside me up to the dais. I was looking down and walking slowly towards the dais. On reaching there, I sat down and around me sat some ladies of Vivaan's family. Few of them I knew beforehand, some were new faces to me whom I was introduced to later. Soon panditji began with reciting out the holy shlokas and hymns to start with the rituals.

In *'God Bharai'*, the bride-to-be was offered gifts, money, jewellery, dry fruits individually by each of the groom's family member. One by one they sat down in front of me and offered me something or the other which after accepting, I kept passing to my mother sitting beside me. Some of my cousins teased me whenever I made an eye contact with any of them. One or two of them kept coming to me again and again and whispered something or the other about Vivaan describing his looks and I could not respond much to them except smiling.

Watching the waiters and vendors going among the people with different sorts of cuisines was mouth watering and I hadn't had anything from the evening. As the eve was proceeding, more and more guests started pouring in. Some ladies on the other side were busy gossiping among themselves and I knew exactly what they would be discussing as how I or Vivaan were looking, how were all the arrangements, did it meet their expectations or not, or even comparing the event to any of their last visited function like this, etc. People like this, you would find in every part of the world.

After the *God Bharai,* finally it was time for the ring ceremony. The stage was cleared for the couple and all the children who had made it their playground were asked to step down. They all screamed in excitement about the ring ceremony and jumped down the stage in no time. Soon I and Vivaan were in front of each other for the very first time on the eve. Among so many relatives and out of shyness,

I was not able to make proper eye contact to him. Our rings were brought by our respective cousins and finally it was the moment I had been waiting for long years.

I might not be able to describe exactly how I felt, but it was like one of your most awaited dreams coming true after you lose hope for everything. But now it was time of rejoicing. As for the ring, mine had a relatively large brilliant cut diamond in the center with small diamonds studded entirely over the platinum band. It was more of Nikhil's choice rather than mine. I also wanted the ring to shine with brilliance and which would look splendid on Vivaan.

I stretched out my hand to Vivaan and like a gentleman's hold, he held my hand in his hand and made me wear the ring. There was a loud applause and claps especially from the youngsters and people showered flowers over us. The DJ also changed his tracks to *'Badhai ho badhai..'*. I was all blushing and felt myself on cloud nine. Then it was my turn to offer the ring to him. He forwarded his hand towards me elegantly. I slipped the ring into his finger and the applause once again. The families also congratulated each other after the ceremony was complete.

Vivaan and I sat on the couch placed on the stage especially designed for the couple on such occasions and people descended the stage to let people take pictures and youngsters encircled around us and sat along with us on the couch itself. People were coming in turns with their families and taking pictures with us turn by turn. The food service had also been started in parallel and some of the lot went to fulfill their tummies. My cousin Daksh, eight years old, kept asking silly questions to Vivaan about ourselves and it seemed like the current and further coming generations would be one step ahead of us all. Office colleagues of both of us also paid us a visit.

Another surprise came from my bestie, Tanshika, when I saw her standing right in front of me. She had made it to the ceremony and explained why she was late due to some official work. I was a bit off with her but after seeing her at the event all that anger vanished in thin air. Soon the DJ dance floor was getting filled with family members and people were dancing to the tunes of all sorts of songs that the DJ played. There were fast paced current generation songs and some of the disco songs of Rishi Kapoor and Mithun. One of Vivaan's uncles was dressed very similar to legendary Bollywood star, Jitendra and people were considering him as his great fan. Some tracks of Jitendra were especially played for him and he imitated Jitendra perfectly. Seeing him rock the dance floor, other members of the family also joined in, mostly of age group 40 and above. It was really a funny and memorable moment to watch your in-laws dancing to the item songs of their time when Jitendra, Mithun, Rishi Kapoor made people dance.

One of my cousins, Ashutosh had developed dance chemistry with one of my in-laws. It was my aunt-in-law Reshma Buaji who was dancing with Ashutosh and the way she rocked the floor was amazing to watch because other ladies of her age were sweating and catching up their breadth after some dance steps. She kept on going and so did Ashutosh. People stopped for a while to watch both of them perform. Meanwhile they also kept conversing over who will stop first and for a moment it didn't seem like there was such an age difference between the two. People gathered around and started hooting and motivating them both. Everyone was laughing out loud hearing their conversation.

Gradually guests started leaving for their homes. I was also feeling hungry but could not express it and so was Vivaan. Then we were also asked to come to the dining area so that our families could also start having dinner. Usually people start with the couple but here, except the family members of both sides, other guests were asked to have their dinner first. Both the families had dinner together and people came to know each other more than before and discussed over numerous matters. Vivaan and I were made to sit in the center table with family members seated around us in respective tables. The focus was more on the couple. Everyone was trying to make sure that the couple's plate was full all the time and they were not eating themselves but feeding each other. The youngsters were giggling every time when I fed Vivaan or he fed me. We talked very less over the table. The dinner was over by 10:30 p.m.

Finally the eve was about to come to an end when after all the guests had left and each of them went with a return gift from my parents as it was a tradition to gift the guests of the evening with something or the other from girl's parents. Everyone gave their blessings once again and it was now time for us to bid goodbye to their family. After Vivaan's family left, we also started for our way back home in pack of six or seven in each of our cars. After we reached home and settled down in our comforts, we started opening gifts which Vivaan's family had given us. I felt sleepy after some time and took leave of everyone and left them with gifts and their talks about the evening.

And just before I was going to sleep, thinking about the whole evening and how everything went so well, I got an SMS. It was from Vivaan. Those words in the message just made my day. It read...

*You were looking really beautiful today. I love you.*

~.~.~.~.~.~.~.~.~.~.~

He asked me to go on a date, a day before he was leaving Kanpur and heading back to Mumbai.

I told him clearly that I wouldn't be going with him on a date without my parent's permission. So he being such a gentle person came to my house on Thursday evening 6'o clock.

He met all of my family members. Then he in-front of my mom and dad said –Mummy Daddy I would like to ask you something?

My mom replied, "Yes? Ask?"

Vivaan, "Can I take Anushree out tonight? I will drop her home safely by 10:30."

Dad said, "Don't you think its wrong to go like this?"

Vivaan, "Dad actually your daughter is so honest and innocent that she will never go without you alls permissions and even I would also not force her to do anything like this. Tomorrow I'm going back to Mumbai. And then would leave for my onsite project to Europe next week. I don't think we'll get time to meet after that. Please dad."

Dad looked at me and asked, "Do you want to go?"

I was so scared and out of my scared positing I replied, "Whatever you say dad!"

Oh no! I should have said yes. Now my dad would say no. And I wouldn't get a chance to go with Vivaan. I was wondering all this and so was Vivaan, as his expressions seemed.

Dad looked at Vivaan with a smile on his face and said, "10:30 sharp?"

Vivaan, full of joy exclaimed, "Yeah sure dad! A gentleman's promise."

I was blank on hearing this. I mean my mom dad permitted me to go on a date! That was so awesome. I was like REALLY?? And soon so many things started popping out of my mind as to

– what am I gonna wear?

-its already 6:30 and we have to come back by 10:30. Only four hours we have and I am still not ready!!

-its my first date so I have to look perfect.

And again I was back to the first question as to what am I gonna wear???

I ran towards my cupboard and took out all of my party wear dresses and smashed them on my bed. When I was trying to figure out what to wear, my mom came in saying, "Can I help?"

"Yeah of-course mummy! You ought to help me out. My dress isn't finalized yet and its already 7. What am I gonna do? We are already late!!"

Mom told me to calm down and sit. She said, "Look... as this is your first date! I would suggest you to wear Vivaan's favourite color and if possible go for that dress which was gifted by Vivaan last month."

"Oh yes! That black midi which he bought for me... he hasn't seen me in that dress yet. I should wear it. What say?"

"Of-course! Go for it my li'l girl".

"You are the best mom in the whole world. I love you mom" I exclaimed and hugged my mom with joy.

"Love you too! Now speed-up else Vivaan would go on a date all alone without you!!", Mom replied and pushed me towards the changing room.

I was ready to go in fifteen minutes. Can you imagine a girl getting ready in just fifteen minutes for her date that too her first date!! I did it. Actually, I wasn't the kind of girl who loves to wear lots of make-up and stilettos. I was a bit different from other girls. Oh no!! its not my verdict but I have heard the same thing from many people and especially Vivaan.

So... soon I was in his car sitting next to him. As it was already fifteen minutes to eight, it was all dark outside.

He took a u-turn. I was puzzled as to where we were going?

I looked at him and said, "Where?"

Vivaan smiled and replied, "This is a kidnap madam!"

"No, seriously tell na? where are we going?"

"Hold on honey... It's a surprise. Till then enjoy this song"

And he played *"tujhme rab dikhta hai"* of the movie *Rab ne bana di Jodi*. Well, this was my most favorite song of which I dreamt a lot. When for the first time I saw this song in the theatre while watching the movie I was on with a jaw-dropped happy expression. And same night, I saw a dream in which I was on a date with a very good looking boy who I saw for the first time and was singing and dancing on the same song. After *"main agar kahoo"* of *Om Shanti Om*, this was my second favourite song which I wanted to re-live in my real life.

I wonder how Vivaan comes to know my most desperate choices and wishes. But whatever it was, he was cute and caring.

So, innocently was he driving the car with one hand on the stearing and other on the gear that I couldn't control myself from looking at him again and again. Although, I wasn't looking at him directly but with side eyes so that he couldn't get an idea that I was trying to gaze him.

Suddenly he said, "Show your hands?"

I while offering my hands to him asked, "Why".

He took my hands upon his, and pressed my hands firmly and said, "You know what? Your hands are really soft. Just like a baby's palms."

Oh my God. Why is he always appreciating me in a way that makes me start blushing. But managing to reply I said, "Thank you."

Vivaan, "Hello! Whose there at the back?"

I surprisingly said, "What are you saying?? Its just the two of us here in the car."

He looked at me and said, "Ohh so you were feeling shy of me? I thought there is somebody else inside this car of whom you are feeling shy." And he giggled hard.

"No there is nothing like that. And by the way, I am not feeling shy and I wasn't blushing."

"It's the joke of the day! Give a round of applause to Miss Anushree", with this line he left the steering and started clapping.

Sometimes I wonder, why these guys try to be funny when actually they are not. Can somebody please tell him that he is not at all funny. Grrr!!

But as it was our first official date, I controlled myself from giving a weird response and tried to give a smile.

Soon, we reached *Ganga-Bairaj*!!

Ahh! The best place in Kanpur. I wonder how places become so special but one sec.! "We are at *Ganga Bairaj*?"

I was totally shocked. I looked at Vivaan with a smile and said, "Thank you."

He did a *googly woogly woksh* on my cheeks and said, Anytime and Anything.

I am in love man!! I am in love!!

He was so romantic. He was so perfect.

Like a gentleman, he ran and opened my door. I stepped out from the car just like a princess holding a hand of her prince charming. It was the perfect evening time. Lights in the *Ganga Bairaj* were so beautifully being reflected from the water of river Ganga. And the most important thing was that this was my all time favourite place.

"You know what Vivaan, you made my evening by bringing me over here. It's my favourite place." I said to him during our walk on the dam.

He clutched his hands with mine and replied – "I know... that is why I have brought you here, to make your evening even more special."

"I always used to wonder, I will visit *Ganga Bairaj* either when it will be the most happiest day or at the most saddest days of my life. I can connect my mind my soul to the most inner self of mine over here. Its like looking myself as the serene child of nature who have seen the time flying on its highest pace."

"You speak so well Anu, why don't you write something? You can be a good writer?"

"Ahh no Vivaan! Not now... But I will... one day... for sure..." I replied leaving his hands and ran to reach the centre of the bridge.

He followed me to the centre of the bridge. It was all dark with the combination of cold breeze. It was only the sound of water which could clearly be heard. I stood by the railing of the bridge to look at the flowing water of the river.

Suddenly I felt warm air near my ears. Although I didn't see what was it but I could feel my heart beats increasing. I turned back, it was Vivaan.

Oh my goodness, we were so close.

He was directly looking into my eyes. Now at these kind of moments, we girls generally don't understand how to react. Infact I myself was very much confused as to move ahead or step back as I was getting a feeling that he was about to kiss me. With all these thoughts in my mind, I was still standing blank and was frozen infront of him.

He held my face with his palms and brought his face near mine. For a second I closed my eyes but out of my nervousness I opened my eyes and exclaimed – "Vivaan I wana tell you something."

He left my face and said, "What?"

He seemed a bit of embarrassed and so was I.

I replied trying to look here and there to avoid looking at him in his eyes, "We should leave now. Its getting late."

He replied, "Okay" and started moving towards the exit.

In the car also, it was all silent.

I didn't know what he was thinking. I was feeling guilty whether I had done something wrong which had resulted in such a situation of silence and we are not getting anything to talk? Should I have let him kiss me which would have resulted in a happier date.

But why did I say that I wanted to tell him something. I am such a confused soul that sometimes I myself am not aware of what I want. I had firmly decided yesterday that I would not be giving that diary to him then why the heck all this?

With the thoughts fighting in my mind and silence prevailing in real in between the two of us, we reached *ChinMi*. *Chinmi* is the best Chinese restro in the town located in Rave 3 and personally my favourite. By the way, its actually Chinmi Not Chimni...

We discussed order to be placed in a very formal way as if he was on a meeting with the client. I mean "What would you like to order ma'am" sounded so formal that I was feeling as if I am with a manager of my company.

Anyhow we placed orders after a long conversation of "no, you tell", "no, your choice" and all that.

And again we both were back on silent mode.

It was getting boring now. Is it a crime to stop a guy from kissing a girl ? Why isn't he speaking anything?

So, being a usual initiator, I said, "Hey tell me something?"

"Yeah?"

"What made you fall in love with me?"

"What kind of a question is this?"

"*Are*, I want to know! Tell na!!"

"Dear, loving someone without a reason is true love and I love you without any reason, so..."

Now this was a shot! But Mr. Vivaan might be wondering that he had a great escape from answering my question. He wasn't knowing that I have a solution for this too.

His smile was telling how proud he was feeling after giving such a diplomatic answer to me. but I smiled too and said, "Okay, falling in love needs no reason! Agreed!! Reason for marrying me?"

Hah!! We girls are always ready with a cross-question to continue and win the argument and his expression was making me feel as I had won a game or something.

He took a deep breath and said, "Ohkay!!! so, you really want to know why I want to marry you?"

I replied, "Yes, apart from the reason that you love me and our parents wants us to get married!"

He was playing with a fork kept on the table and suddenly he kept it aside and sat attentively. He trying to make an eye contact with me said, "See, you are the one whom I have loved since I was a small child. Previously when I wasn't knowing that what exactly love is, I just used to admire you, gaze you, follow you and wanted to talk to you when we were in school. When you left our school and went to Delhi with your family, then I missed you... When we again met that day and I got confirmed that you are the same Anushree Sharma whom I have loved and missed since so many years, I was on cloud nine. And that very moment I had fallen for you very deeply and I realised whatever I had felt in my past and in absence, it was love... Everytime I missed you, I told Vansh," continued Vivaan, "Vansh, you remember??"

I replied, "Yeah the tallest guy of our class?"

"Yeah, exactly !! So, Vansh used to say that it is next to impossible to meet you again in life... and I would be really lucky to find you! We both searched you on social networking sites and found you nowhere... he also said that it is quite possible that you must be in a relationship with some one else as after all you were in Delhi. And being in a relation is quite common especially for a 'ten on ten' girl like you. But deep within me, there was a faith that No, you wont be having any relationship with anyone."

I have that blind trust in you. I have that feeling that I know you very well, I know each and everything about you. I have a faith in me that like you are the first girl in my life and I am also the first guy in your life. I always wanted to be the first and last guy in your life!! You are just my kind of girl..."

"Ahm, excuse me sir", said the waiter as he interrupted our conversation. This break was really needed. I mean I wasn't getting how to react what to say. I said, "Excuse-me and went to the washroom."

Standing by the mirror, I was looking into my eyes and trying find out the answer of what?

This guy trusts me like anything. I mean what????

He believes whatever he thinks... and he hated liars. Now what should I do? I have to give him that diary to read. That diary about my past life.

But what if he breaks our relation our marriage after reading all that truth about me? But I cant break his trust by keeping him in hidden and unknown of the reality. What if he comes to know from somewhere else?

I have to risk it.

*Sins were mine, and so shall I have to pay for it...*

I finally decided that I would give that diary to him. Thereafter whatever happens, whatever may be Vivaan's decision, I would accept it happily.

I returned back to the table. Vivaan seemed to be waiting impatiently for my return.

As soon as I got seated Vivaan asked, "What happened? Is all fine?"

I replied trying to manage a smile, "Yeah, all is fine. Vivaan, I want to give you something?'

He replied excitingly, "Yes sure? What?"

"Not today ! Tomorrow !! Okay?"

"Yeah, fine... so we are going to meet tomorrow again! Thank you so much."

He was serving our food and I was just looking at him. He seemed so happy and relaxed. His smile was so soothing that I couldn't let my eyes off from him. Just one thing was grooving over my mind was I wish this moment stops here only, no future to look forward, no past to worry about. Just this moment of us prevails forever.

Vivaan interrupted me and said, "What happened? You all-right?"

"Can I say something?"

"Sure Anu!!"

"Vivaan, I love you a lot. No matter what happens tomorrow, I will always want you to be happy", I said with tears in my eyes. I was feeling as if this was the last time I was sitting with him happily. As there were more chances of Vivaan leaving me after reading my diary!!

"Love you too dear,! Hey... why are you crying???", asked Vivaan holding my hands tightly.

"No just like that... for the first time I am having a feeling that I Love you with all my heart and soul... so... anyways leave..."

I wiped my tears off and soon we started dining...

Like a good son-in-law, Vivaan kept his promise and dropped me home by 10:20 p.m.

All night I was just wondering about the date. It was all so perfect.

But if on one hand I was happy for the date which we had, on the other hand I was damn scared cause of my diary and his reaction.

Actually if it would not have been Vivaan, if it would have been some other guy whom I was getting married to, I would have never thought this much... about telling him my past stories and experiences... but as it was Vivaan, he loved me since childhood... and even I had fallen for him so deeply, I had to follow my principle of life and I had to tell him the whole story...

Many a time I thought of cancelling this idea but everytime he said that he is the first guy in my life, although it was true but then only one thing came in my mind not telling him about my past would be a bigger lie and would be like breaking his faith and trust. So, I decided that this is the right to time to tell him each and everything thing.

Tomorrow I would give him the diary...

Rest god would handle!!

# 6

# Duh-Oh, Fate!

Vivaan had to leave Kanpur by 3 p.m. anyhow. As it takes almost two hours to reach Amausi airport from Kanpur and if God's grace is high and traffic jams near Unnao then three to four hours.

It was already 12 noon. My phone was continuously ringing from Vivaan's call as we decided to meet at 11 in CCD, Mall Road. One of the finest located CCDs in Kanpur.

I don't know if this is the problem with all girls or I am the special one but Full night I was thinking about the date and moments which we had spent, then I was wondering as to how he would react after reading my diary. Would he leave me forever or would he accept me with the reality of mine. And the whole night passed. I remember I saw the watch when it struck 5. I in great hurry kept the watch aside and thought of taking a nap till 10. Then one hour to get ready and then all the way to CCD.

Everything was so perfect... But this sleep of mine ruined it all. I woke up at 12 with my mom's voice.

Oh my God!! What shall I do now. But still, I got ready again in half an hour. Picked up Vivaan's call, not giving him a moment to speak I immediately said, "I am coming, I am coming. Just give me ten mintues." And I smashed the phone inside my scooty's dicky.

Riding any vehicle on the roads of Kanpur is actually a big deal for a person who doesn't now belong to this place. There is a common proverb for Kanpur and its traffic "If you can drive in Kanpur you can drive anywhere in the world".

I don't know whether I should feel proud of it or feel embarrassed ... choice is mine so I chose to feel proud of it. We here in Kanpur provide driving experts to whole of India. Driving in extreme conditions with ruthless traffic and dangerous roads makes a man perfect in driving.

I was enjoying my ride to the fullest with my Philips go-gear on playing "*Here I am, this is me*" of Bryan Adams.

Suddenly my scooty started to boggle.

Now what???

From 50 speed, my scooty reduced to 0.

What the heck is this?

Oh no, its puncture. I don't have time for this. I decided to call a nearby friend and hand over my scooty to her. It was already 1 'o clock. I was already late.

Shit man!! Listening to the song "*It's a new world, it's a new day*..." I was wondering how nothing could go wrong and see!! My plans never work.

I called Shitie, my friend from guitar class to take my scooty to a *puncture-wala* and get it repaired. I told her to take it home, I shall pick it from her home only after my meeting.

I booked an auto for Mall Road, city centre. These stupid *auto-walas* are also on a look for the correct situation. It seems as if they seek desperate customers so that they can charge whatever they want. I was in a real hurry so I decided to pay 75 bucks to this stupid guy who was actually feeling proud after convincing me to pay him 75 bucks for 2.5 freaking kilometers.

His face was telling as if he has won an award or something. But I decided not to ruin my mood just because of this creep. I focused on the watch. Time was really running faster than ever. Everything was so messed up. I was holding my cellphone, my mp 3 players, handsfree of my cellphone and money in one hand and on the other, it was my diary, a wallet, a stole, and my shades.

It was 1:30 when I reached the Mall.

I payed him the money in a hurry and started running towards the Mall's entrance.

My stole got stuck in the door. I was trying to take it out with force and as it came out, I banged into a lady standing behind me.

From where the hell this lady came and why the hell was she standing behind me. I felt like shouting on her but then I controlled myself and decided to focus on the things which we both dropped.

"Oh my God!! My Phone... My Go gear... Cant you see and walk?", I said furiously.

"I am really sorry girl... I came to help you. Saw you struggling with your stole stuck in this door", replied that girl in a very easy tone.

"I am sorry, I dropped all your books and diaries", I replied in a very pissed –off tone.

We picked and handed over each others stuff and moved away.

Meanwhile Vivaan came walking inside the CCD.

"Are you alright?", he asked me in a worry-full tone.

"Yeah.. I am fine now! Lets go..."- I replied.

We came in CCD and got seated.

"What happened Anu? we were supposed to meet at 11. And its 2 o' clock. I called you up so many times but u didn't respond." Vivaan was as expected ready with his list of questions.

"Yeah.. phone was inside the scooty's dicky!!" I replied while making myself comfortable on the sofa.

"Where is your scooty????" inquired Vivaan.

"Yaar, what to tell... it got punctured." Gosh, I was so much pissed-off !!

"So, you left it there only? You should have called me up", suggested Vivaan.

"No –No! I called Shitie.. she took it for repairing."

"Ohh!!! Are you alright?" said Vivaan as he called the waiter by waving his hands.

"Yeah... I am fine... just feeling a bit pissed-off!!" I said.

"Coffee?" asked him.

"Yeah sure.." as I replied Vivaan ordered coffee for two of us to the waiter standing next to him.

"So...? Where is my gift?" asked Vivaan excitingly.

"Its not a gift actually... but yes... here it is!" and I handed over that diary to him.

Before he could open the diary I stopped him.

"Please no!!! Not here in front of me..."

"But why", he tried to make a sad face.

"Just like that... open it when I am gone..." I said... I did not want him to see that diary in front of me. For then, I had to answer his long list of questions about the diary!

"Okay...", he replied.

"By the way, thanks to this diary.. because of this only you met me today... else.."

"Yeah yeah I know..." I said while sipping my coffee.

This ended our conversation. As I was getting nervous about wondering of his reaction after reading this diary, I couldn't find any conversation starter this day.

But still, I had to because it was our last happy meeting as I wasn't knowing how he would react when he would read my diary. Whether he would stop talking to me, break our relation or he would just let past go and carry our relation forward towards marriage. According to my perception, I always took the negative scenario first as it helped a person to prepare himself for the worst thing in life and makes a person more strong.

With "So... all set?" I again initiated. What the heck dude!!! Why can't I sit silently like other people. Why is there always a conversation going on when I am there. I really need to change this habit of mine.

He said, "Yeah.. all set..! so, when are we meeting next?"

"Depends on you!!" – I replied sadly.

"May be after 6 or 7 months... I just hope everything remains the same as today..."

His voice sounded as if he was upset or feeling something which he was unable to express.

Of-course this feeling was obvious, he was going for a long time and quite possible that we would not be able to be in contact like we are today.

With the thoughts clustering in my mind, I was sitting silently.

Suddenly for a change he asked, "Hey when are your end semester exams gonna start?"

"May be next week. I don't have any idea", I said casually.

"So when are you going back to Lucknow?" he asked.

"Tomorrow!!" I replied sadly. I was really sad... I never liked living in lucknow and I hated when I had to go back and live in that god forbidden hostel.

We smiled at each other. Finished our coffee...

It was the time to say goodbye.

I was getting a feeling that this might be my final goodbye from his life.

So, for the first time I hugged him very tightly that it brought tears in my eyes.

I whispered in his ears 'I really love you Vivaan'.

He kissed me on my forehead and said, "Love you too, take care!"

We both were sad and apparently we both didn't want us to part our ways... we wanted to be together forever... but we had to go...

He dropped me at Shitie's residence and went away...

I saw him going far away till he took a turn and disappeared from my vision. I couldn't stop myself from bursting out into tears.

Somewhere within me, I was getting a feeling of regret that I shouldn't have given that diary to him. When all was going well in our lives then why did I take that decision.

And somewhere I was feeling that whatever I decided was right. That person is the one whom I am going to get married with, he has a right to know each and everything about me and if he isn't aware of the truth then it my duty to tell him all things right away.

One hour passed.

Vivaan called me up –'Hey!'

"Hello..."- I immediately picked up the phone because I was waiting for his call desperately.

"Dear, I didn't understand why you gave me this diary?"- said Vivaan.

I was puzzled to hear this and so replied- "Why, what happened?"

"I mean, it's a blank diary!"

What.....?????? A blank diary!!!!! How on earth is this possible????

I mean I wrote it myself and it was full and then he is saying it's a blank diary?

Its just not possible. He must be kidding. So I inquired- "Are you sure? You must be kidding right?"

"No Not at all... why will I joke about this? I myself am confused as to why you gave me a blank diary!! I saw sitting in my cab, on way to airport. So, I thought of giving an over-view to your diary. When I opened it, it was all blank pages. So, immediately I called you up" said Vivaan.

I was astonished to hear this and couldn't believe how was it possible.

"Vivaan, there might be a mistake. Have you checked it properly?" I again asked Vivaan.

"Yes, Anu off-course..." Vivaan said and he seemed surprised too.

"Vivaan, I will call you back in a minute." And I smashed the phone. Ran towards my cupboard to find out whether I took the correct diary or not. But no diary was there. Of course, how can I make such a big mistake. I checked it properly when I took it out from my scooty at the time of switching from the scooty to auto.

What was happening?

I was totally puzzled.

I called him back – "hey".

"Yes, Anu? What happened?", said Vivaan.

"Well, you sure *na*, its all blank in that diary?", I again inquired as it was really hard to grasp this.

"Yeah.. by the way, what was there in that diary?? Anything serious???" I was trying to avoid this question but... ultimately I had to face it. Now say what was there in that diary."

Due to a reflex-action, suddenly a thought came in my mind.

May be it was God's wish that Vivaan shouldn't read that diary and shouldn't know about my past life?

May be its all planned somewhere in the heaven that when all is going well then why you are creating such a nuisance by giving this diary so God made it lost or vanished?

I know, these thoughts are kind of weird to accept but I, being highly spiritual person always had these kind of thoughts in all the weird situations.

I replied – "Naah!! Nothing serious... just wanted to show my writings to you. Once you told na, that you want to see my writings and compositions. Thats why... leave it..."

"Ohhkay!! No worries... when I will return from my trip... then I would read your other works. Till then keep writing." He sounded more relaxed.

"Yeah, sure... anyways.. happy journey." I said.

"Yeah. Thanks... take care. Bye" replied Vivaan, and we disconnected the call.

Although, I talked to him in a very bubbly way trying to show off that the diary thing wasn't a serious part but in my mind I was really tensed and wondering where on earth that diary disappeared.

Then gave a thought –if its gone... let it go. Neither I can write that 300 page diary again nor can I bring it back with magic. So, let it be...

May be its our destiny.. atleast I tried my level best and made efforts to tell each and everything to Vivaan. Now if the diary itself is lost, nothing can be done.

So, I decided to forget this diary incidence although it was not at all easy... but still I tried to... and also tried to focus on my end semester exams which were probably going to be started from the next week...

# 7

# Life Changed

Months passed.

It was Feb 20. I was in the last semester of my Masters in Journalism and Mass Communication. Being in the final semester, it was the time of internship and I was still unemployed.

Actually, my resume or pointers were not a reason for my unemployment as I was a good and consistent student who always scored 8+ pointers, problem was my confusion. I being a BBA graduate switched to Masters in Journalism and Mass Communication just for sake of a post graduate degree. In addition to it, I also wanted to be a corporate communication specialist at the time when I joined this course. But time passed, semesters passed and my confusion of what actually I wanted to be increased.

Basically, I wanted to become a writer but after joining MJMC in Amity University, I came to know the aspects of print media. Teachers were more emphasized on teaching the hard-core journalism rules and the print media industry rather than trying to teach what exactly a student wants to be taught about.

They taught us all the subjects like Journalism, Print media, Electronic media -TV and radio, Public relations, Advertising etc. etc.

Like me, I met few other students who rolled in to be a news presenter, TV anchor, VJ or RJ. Everybody was more into entering bollywood or glamour world but nobody wanted to be a hardcore journalist. And so, I was one of them. Every semester we were taught new subjects which were of course very interesting and which also helped in making the students more confused about our specialisation.

And so, till the month of Feb came, I was totally confused about my internship and specialisation and so, I was at my home in Kanpur taking a short break from all this confusion and planning of what to do next.

I informed my college that I was going out of station for fifteen days for my brother's marriage and luckily as it was the last semester and we were not being tortured and blackmailed of getting debarred and being punished for not attending classes. So, luckily I was granted with leave.

While I was busy playing with my fluffy white and super cute puppy, Rony, my phone rang.

It was a call from an unknown number.

I ignored it and decided to continue playing with my Rony.

But that call was like testing my patience.

The person called me up continuously and so, my mom ordered me either to pick the call or to switch my phone off.

I choose to receive it.

"Hello", I spoke in a very annoyed tone.

In return I heard a very sweet voice of a girl, she said, "Hi... is it Anushree?"

"Yes, may I know whose calling?" I replied.

"Anushree Sharma??", she inquired.

"Yes..?"

"Hi Anushree, I am Saira Khan calling from SS Publications, New Delhi."

"Yeah hi... So??"- I immediately lowered my tone and spoke. I thought she called me up to offer a job or something... I usually got calls like this and so I thought it to be one amongst them only.

"Well, we have met before." She said.

"Amm when? Sorry I can't recall..." – I said trying to recognize her.

She said trying to make me remember the incident "Well, Anushree you remember some months back I guess in December, we banged into each other in the Mall and we both dropped our stuff." she continued "and you were in hurry and so you went away without checking your stuff??"

"Ohh yeah yeah... so, from where did you got this number?". Now this was really weird. I was getting a bit of idea but my mind wasn't ready to accept it without the clear picture of the whole scenario.

"Well, ma'am do you remember you wrote a diary. A Green color diary??"

"Oh yes!!! Is it with you???"- I wasn't knowning how to react to this. I mean after a span of approximately three months, this girl named Saira Khan is calling me and telling me about my diary.

Now what was the matter. Why now? Why not before?

"Yes, its with me. Well, I really apologize for not returning you that diary at that time. Actually, when I reached my place... I saw your diary... read starting pages of it and found it very interesting. So I decided to read the whole diary. Its really nice story I must say and I am sorry again that I read your personal diary." She sounded really sweet when she said all that but on hearing this I just got out of my nerves.

"So, now will you please send me my diary back?", I replied in a very angry tone. Oh come on she read my personal diary? And now she is calling back and telling me that she liked the story? The story? I mean is she serious? Its my personal diary. I felt like shouting on her but first I decided to hear what she called me for?

She replied, "Ma'am here's my point of calling you. I being an editor in a publishing house, read your story, crossed checked it and sent it for editorial evaluation. Your diary is actually a potential novel and I am sure it can be amongst the bestselling novels when published. I just wanted your permission to publish it as it is your diary, your writing and you story...".

"No. not at all... oh please... it is not a fictional story which you are willing to publish. It is all full with my life's incidents. You have no idea what you are planning." I strictly ordered her.

"Ma'am, I understand but who knows it's a reality or a fictional novel?" She tried to convince me. Gosh, I must say she was really stubborn and demonstrated strong journalism traits in her.

But I was sure, was this kind of joke going on... I was firm that I didn't want it to get published so I replied "No ways!! Please.. I want the diary back. I will text you my address, just courier it back to me".

"Ma'am, take some time to think about this. I will get back to you after a week. And if still you didn't agree then for sure I will return your diary back to you. Thanks and bye!!" And she disconnected the call.

What the heck man!!!

What was this????

I mean... I was totally blank. What to do what not to.

One side, I was trying to feel happy as an opportunity knocked my door on its own, but on the other side, it was my diary. How on earth can I get it published.

I told my mom the whole story...

I rang up Tanshika, and two more of my friends and narrated the whole scene.

And to my surprise, everybody was happy to hear this and suggested me to agree to this offer.

Now how can everybody agree to this offer. It was not a fictional story which could be published. It was my life's reality.

Please somebody come and support me... but actually, even one side of my own thoughts did not support. They wanted to believe in Saira Khan's vision – "Who knows it's the reality or fiction".

I never ever thought life would bring me to such a crossroad where one side it's my dream and other side it's my life. I had to choose somehow. And so, as all suggested... I finally agreed to Saira's proposal.

I called her up and told about the flip of my decision. I was wondering that the way I said no to her rudely, she would never ever talk to me again and neither would she now publish my book. But to my surprise, she was damn polite when I talked to her. She actually burst out into laughing and said - "I must say Anushree, you are really mature in your writings but in reality you are still a kid!!"

She told me all the norms of the publication house, which were just a kind of formality.

I signed the bond and accepted the royalty rules.

I never knew my dream of being a writer would come true in such an unexpected way.

I titled my book *"Before Saying Sorry..."* Made some changes and wrote the prologue and epilogue.

Finally from my part, all things were done. And so I was free from the publication's side.

The publication house told me that it would take approximately six months to get the novels published.

I decided not to tell about my debut novel to anyone accept those who already knew and who helped me in deciding should I get it published or not. Not even Vivaan knew about his novel.

Time passed... I finished with my MJMC somehow.

Got many offers from the magazines and newspapers to join in as a content editor or the assistant editor but I chose the most unexpected and different thing.

I chose to be a photographer in a well known lifestyle magazine in Delhi.

Actually I was waiting for my novel to be published and I had decided to continue being a writer throughout my life. I found photography as my side-carrier and something which was interesting to pursue too.

I also got offers from some local newspapers and magazines so I started writing columns for them also.

It was all good.

As six months had passed, it was time for Vivaan to return to India from his on-site project in Europe.

Who knew time for my novel's release and Vivaan's come back would clash on the date of his birthday.

It was August 20, Vivaan's birthday and my book release in Delhi.

Co-incidentally, Vivaan was also to land on the same day in the same city. So, I told him to catch me up straight away in the Taj hotel's lobby at 1:30 that day.

He had no idea what he was about to see when he will be reaching there.

If I would have been in his place, I would have thought of a surprise party thrown for me on my birthday by my boyfriend or fiancée.

But the scene was entirely different and highly unexpected.

He called me when he reached Taj which was situated in the Cantt area of Delhi.

I told him to come inside, to the Shahjahan hall in the basement. He was continuously asking me what was going on but I didn't want to break such a big surprise so I controlled my excitement and told him to shut his mouth and come right away.

I can't forget his expressions when he entered the hall.

He was in a jaw-dropped situation standing numb, as if he was in between the aliens from outer space.

I went near him and hugged him.

All the invited reporters and photographers started clicking our snaps.

He was totally numb and speechless.

I whispered in his ear, "Surprise... Happy birthday sweet-heart. I missed you a lot."

He looked at me and said, "What is all this Anu??"

Now what kind of a reply was this?

I was definitely expecting something else rather than this.

I replied, "It a book launch event."

"Whose book?" he seemed really shocked.

"Mine", I laughed and said.

"What??? Your book? When did you write a book? You didn't tell me?? I mean you should have...??" Vivaan was surely running short of words. I mean everybody would..!!

"Okay relax!! I thought of giving you a surprise. That's why did not told you." I replied as I hugged Vivaan.

"Surprise or a shock!!!" - now his expressions were quite confusing. One moment I thought he is happy but surprised and on the other he seemed to be very angry and shocked.

"Please relax... So many people are here for this event. Don't behave in such a weird manner."

On hearing this, he hugged me tightly and said, "Congratulations *beta*. You cant imagine how happy I am right now. Thank you for this gift. It's the best thing I could ever get".

Ohkay... Now he was back to normal and back to his senses.

The book launch event was successfully done.

I was in the list of authors officially now. My facebook account and my inbox both were oozing with congratulation messages.

It seemed hard for some of the people to believe that I was a novelist now and this reflected in their comments and behaviour too. Especially some of my jealous friends from Amity and some relatives!!

Me and Vivaan celebrated his birthday together with my novel's release celebration.

Soon I was back to Kanpur for some work and he to Mumbai.

I gifted him with the complimentary copy of my novel and forced him to read it as soon as possible.

Vivaan being an investement banker usually was really a busy guy, busy in his number crunching and stock updates and hardly got time to read novels. Also he was least interested in reading novels... he found them boring and time-consuming!!

But as it was my book, he somehow managed to...

I gave him a month's time to read it.

He accepted to read and promised to complete the novel within a month. Every night after our phone conversation he read my book for at least half an hour...

# 8

# Before Saying Sorry

The only mistake of mine was that I never had courage to accept the truth...

I am just a simple and innocent girl who never got a chance to express herself and this is my story.

So, *Before saying sorry* to god, to myself and to all of you whom I have hurt, I would like to tell you all the story of my life, till date...

It was the year of 2001 when I left school and Kanpur after passing out the sixth standard, I moved to Delhi with my family. There I got admitted in the school named D.A.V.

It was the new city, new people, new atmosphere and so were the things...

At that time we only had landline phones and no personal cellphones were there like today, I lost contacts with most of my buddies of old school.

Till the time, I was in my old school, I never had even thought of leaving that place and those friends so never thought of exchanging numbers and making long lasting promises to be in contact through letters and all that. Things happened so suddenly that I didn't get time to even say a goodbye to them.

March exams ended, then summer vacations started, in between that only my dad got transferred to Delhi and soon we means me and my family was in Delhi.

But still I had numbers of two three girls of my class who lived nearby my home in Kanpur.

So, I tried to be in touch with them and others too by having talks like please convey my hi to him or her.

Life moved on. In this new school of mine, I made new friends and enemies too.

There was a guy in my class named Kush Ahuja. He was an ugly looking tall guy. I never understood what exactly was his problem. From the day one, he always tried to underestimate and dominate me. He used to taunt me infront of teachers and I really hated this.

He used to call me a small town girl in front of the whole class. But reason behind his hatred was unknown to me till we reached class ten.

There was also a guy named Shahid, he was damn cute and adorable. Just like a perfect guy with perfect looks and personality.

Me and Shahid soon started sitting together and soon became good buddies.

He used to help me through my homework and even class-work.

He was a bright student so, he was also popular amongst the teachers.

With his popularity, I too became popular and was made the class prefect within a month only. Co-incidence was that till now, Kush was the class prefect, now his badge was owned by me so automatically, his level of hatred for me was raised by ten bars.

I tried to talk to him many times and tried to find out what was his problem with me, but whenever I approached him to talk he humiliated me infront of all...

Many a time, he made me cry because of his behavior so finally, after trying a lot I decided to ignore him and stop noticing his behavior.

Time passed, we were in class ten and things were still the same except that Shahid had started liking and praising me.

I too liked Shahid but only as a friend.

Now this line is said by most of the girls at the time when they have to reject a guys proposal. But according to me, the fact is that its an understood and default thing, when we like someone, then only we are friends with that someone. If we dislike a person then we would never ever had talked to him. For example, me and Kush. Kush disliked me, and so he behaved in such a rude manner always when we were around.

And I liked Shahid and his company, so we used talk a lot and spend most of the time together.

I started getting an idea that Shahid had started looking out for me and had fallen for me.

We were growing up and so were our thoughts and perception.

Our class buddies started teasing us for each other. Whenever Shahid was named, others took my name too. May it be the school quire team, dance group or the project partners.

I started finding it suffocating as I took Shahid just like my best buddy.

It was the last board exam, when Shahid finally proposed to me.

He had brought a card for me, a big red colored card with red roses made on it all over and "I LOVE YOU" written on it several times.

If I would have loved him then according to me, it would have been the best ever thing which happened to me. But problem was that I wasn't in love with him. But being his best friend I didn't want to loose him and also didn't want to hurt him. So I was in a big dilemma, so decided to ask for some time to think.

Shahid's reply in this reference was, "Take your time dear... I can wait for my whole lifetime".

Quite touchy and filmy too. Can a person love a person in such a way with so much passion in reality?

Answer was still doubtful for this question as I till the time couldn't believe that I am so good that a person could fall in love with me.

I mean Delhi girls grow up very soon and start to look like a diva in their early age. I was not-so-good-looking normal girl who loved to get dressed up in a pair of blue denims and t-shirts.

Even my hair were always unmanaged and tangled.

So, it was quite difficult for me to accept this thing.

One of my good friend Kriti was a true diva. She used to get proposals every week and was like a role model to me.

No doubt she was gifted with attractive looks and good personality, so her case was normal but not mine.

I took suggestions from many of the friends about this matter as this was my life's first proposal ever..

On one of side, I was unable to believe that I was really that good that a guy like Shahid could fall for me and on the other side, I was feeling pity for him because of his one-sided infatuation or may be love.

In schools, a girl was supposed to be like a typical *behenji* if she had not got any proposals.. Rule was that Only Divas get proposals.

So, many suggested to accept it, while many to reject and many many acted like a media and spread this news of his proposal to me all over..

Next day I was welcomed in the school by so many congrats and hugs.

And I was clarifying to all that there was nothing like that.

It was the day of my chemistry practical, the last practical after which my summer vacations would start. I thought of passing this day without talking to anyone and so would be able to escape the situation of answering Shahid's proposal. But something else was there round the corner. A very unexpected thing happened.

I was preparing for the viva after my practical in the fourth floor of the building, sitting all alone on the staircase.

Kush came.

In a vigorous tone he asked "I have heard something about you and Shahid, is it true?"

I was totally shocked. I mean this moron always humiliated and underestimated me since my day one in school and after four years finally he came by himself to me, just to ask this?

I replied surprisingly replied – "What????????????????"

He said agressively, "Don't act as if you are not aware?"

"And you don't act as if you really care?" I replied with attitude.

"Answer my question Anushree!!". His look was getting furious.

"I don't know what you have heard, but there is nothing in between me and Shahid. I take him just as a friend and he loves me. he has proposed to me and I have asked for sometime to think".

"Say no to his proposal" he said, turned back and started moving away.

"Excuse me???" I shouted.

I stood up and tried to stop him then and there.

He looked into my eyes and said, "Very seriously I am warning you, say no to him".

"But why?" I asked.

"See, I don't think it is important for me to answer your silly series of whys. Just do as I say".

Now these were heights.

I mean how can you order me to take decision of my life. Who are you? I Was feeling like pushing him from that floor or thrashing him hard but I controlled my anger and replied, "Kush, what is the matter?"

Kush turned back, looked into my eyes and said "You want to know what matter is? Alright."

"Listen, I may sound silly or weird to you but I love you since I have seen you for the first time, since your day one in school. I fought with myself and with you too to avoid this feeling as I don't think I am a boy who is a boyfriend material because of my attitude and weird nature. So, I wanted you to hate me, but when this son of a bitch proposed to you and I realized that I can't see you with anyone else in this world. You are mine and you will always remain mine forever till the end and I can fight with anyone to get you in my life."

His eyes were red and face was full of anger. I was so scared after listening this that I was actually shivering.

He left me after saying all this and went away.

I was standing like a statue on the staircase with a blank mind trying to come out from the trance situation, back to reality to understand what actually happened.

What the heck was this. Was this a dream? Or actually a night-mare!!!

This guy came in, proposed to me with lots of threatning sentences and then went away. And this psycho thinks that I would say no to Shahid for his sake.

Previously I was planning to say no to Shahid but now just for the sake of Kush's threats to me, I decided to accept Shahid's proposal.

That day only, I said yes to Shahid.

Vacations passed. Board results were good but only for me. I secured 72 per cent and so got a personal cellphone as a gift but on the other hand, Shahid failed and so he left the school. He decided to join his family business of import and export.

Now, we all were in class eleven. I was all alone to face Kush's reaction as now there was no Shahid to protect me there. I didn't tell my and Kush's conversation to anyone. Not even to my best friend Kriti.

First day of the school was normal as Kush was absent and he remained absent for few days more.

Mine and Shahid's conversation graph was also decreasing day by day because of his business pressures.

Kush was also a changed guy now.

He had stopped talking to everyone. I also heard that he became a ciggrette addict too. Every now and then he had fights with the guys inside and outside the school. Previously he was a topper but now he became just an average student.

But I also decided to stay away from him. But life –the highly unpredictable journey had something else for me in store.

By the way, let me mention I hate co-incidences because they are not planned, truly unwanted and especially those which are not in my favour.

For a science model competition, me and Kush were made partners in the biology project as he scored the highest in the board exams followed by me.

Gosh!! Not all good marks and good results are actually good for you.

As this was school's vice-principal's decision so, even faculty could not help us.

The given topic was "Production of bio-ethanol from sugar cane" and for that we had to visit a sugar-cane industry situated at the outskirts of Ghaziabad.

If god would have granted me one wish that day, I would have chosen to become invisible.

It means me and Kush for a full one day industrial visit 80 kms away from school and the main city and above all – all alone.

How on earth was this gonna happen.

A day before our industrial visit, vice-principal called both of us to the office.

She gave a very nice and very motivational lecture on we have to win, its about our school's pride, give your best and all that. And the only thing in my mind was am I really going with him tomorrow?

When we both came out of the office, Kush said – tomorrow 7 o'clock in the morning I will pick you from the school's gate. Be there on time.

How expressionless was he looking. And he didn't wait for my reply. Just said his words and went away. How mean!! I mean, he always does this; Spits out his words and goes away without listening to my answer.

Felt like slapping him and telling him to wake up from his sleep and try to be a bit realistic and professional.

But as usual he was gone and I was left alone with my controlled feelings.

I called Shahid to tell him the whole stuff but he was busy. He didn't pick up my call and in return he texted me – sweet-heart, I am busy in a meeting and this whole week would be busy. Call you when free and don't wait for my call. Take care. Xoxo.

Next day morning I reached school at 6:30 and he was there just five minutes after me.

He had brought his Hyundai Accent car. Oh my god!! Can he drive? As I had an image of his like a typical villain in my mind. I was feeling uncomfortable to sit in with him. I was getting weird thoughts like–what if he kidnapped me? what if he caught hold of me by my neck and ask me to say yes to him or what if he willingly banged his car with a tree to murder me and all that.

Someone has rightly said, 'Girls are really very complicated and they are aware of this fact very well.'

He opened the front door and said, "Ma'am will you please sit in?"

I silently sat inside the car.

He was listening to an old song "*aye zindagi gale laga le*" from *Sadma* and guess what? He turned off the music player as I stepped inside the car. I mean how rude!!!

I felt like telling him that I am not a music-allergic person and for his kind information this song was one of my favourites but then again... I chose to remain silent.

After half an hour of drive, he asked, "Did you have your breakfast?"

As it was highly unexpected I replied "What?"

"Breakfast?"

"Amm no!!"

He again asked "Are you hungry??"

And I answered his question by asking, "Are you hungry??"

He replied, "I asked first?"

And I replied, "I, second!!"

And we both laughed.

It was quite weird. We both were talking and laughing?

Again it was silence in between us as I realised that I was with Kush!!!

After five minutes he said, "so?"

I giving a puzzled expression replied, "SOo??"

"Madam, when you start feeling hungry, do let me know!!"

"Why?" now this was actually stupid. After saying this I realized that I should have said okay instead...

"Well, we eat something then?"

"Ohh okay" I tried to give him a smile but this guy wasn't looking at me so my attempt of being friendly and my smile, both went in vain.

After a small silence, I thought of starting a conversation. And till date I don't know why I did that.

I asked, "So... are you really interested in participating in this science model competition?"

"No!!" he firmly replied.

"Why?"

He gazed at me for a second, took a deep breath and said, "Why do you always have a why ready after almost every sentence of mine?"

"I am sorry"- I replied and started looking out of the window.

After a while, we stopped at a *dhaba*.

I was amazed to hear him asking me, "You like coffee na? should I order one for you?"

I was like, "How do you know that I like coffee??????"

But I said, "Yeah sure..."

We sipped our coffees and had French fries silently.

He asked, "Anything else you want?"

I said, "Yeah, take a mineral water bottle."

He replied okay and told me to go back to the car.

He again like a gentleman opened the door for me. we both stepped in, he handed over the water bottle to me and again we were on the way to the factory.

It was something strange, something was happening in between us. Or may be it was my illusion. But all through my thoughts just one thing was going through –Kush, you are not that bad. I am sorry for misunderstanding you.

I was feeling curious to know what he felt for me at that time.

Were we friends by that time???

We remained silent throughout the visit. The only conversation prevailed in between us was "Are you hungry?" "Do you want anything?" "Are you comfortable?" "Do you have any problem" and so on...

I was unclear was it his real care or just the formalities.

But things were different now. We had almost spent a whole day together. Had breakfast, lunch, series of coffees and cold drinks... we discussed about our project... and I felt that my hesitation of speaking to him was gone.

He was actually not that bad...

He dropped me at my home's nearest bakery. It was approx half kms. away from my home in Kailash sectors.

When I was just about to step out of the car, he interrupted, "Anushree??"

I sat back – "Yes??"

"Can I ask you something???", he said.

"Yeah sure..!!"

"Do you really love Shahid??", he asked me looking straight into my eyes.

Now this was really not expected. I mean... even I never asked this question to myself. May be I never thought of it too. I mean yes, he was my boyfriend but did I actually love him? We never had a boyfriend - girlfriend kind of a conversation too!! And most importantly, I just said yes to him because of Kush's sudden proposal and my anger. So... it was clear, my answer was no.

I avoided to look back into his eyes and replied, "He is my boyfriend Kush!!"

"Look at me. My question is, do you love him or not???"

He was making me nervous and scared again. Oh My God.. why do I always have to face such kind of situations. Please make me invisible god... please...

I replied, "Kush... its getting late. Can I go??"

"Okay. Got your answer.. You may go now, bye!!", he said.

I stepped out of the car wondering what he got? I mean I don't love him. This is well known to me. How can he understand this? He must be thinking that I love him a lot and all that. I decided to clarify to him all the things and the present scenario.

I decided to talk to him on this matter after the science model competition.

On the day of the competition, when results were about to get declared. We both were standing near the stage.

As it was declared that our model has won the second prize, we hugged each other tightly with joy.

After few seconds we both realised that we were actually hugging each other, we both moved away.

Went to the stage, took the prize together. Clicked for pictures for the newspapers.

We were the second winners and so we were very happy.

I really thought that we can be good friends together, so I approached him to talk to him about me and Shahid.

We sat down on a round table.

I started the conversation with, "See... first let me complete whatever I want to say, then you may speak."

He agreed with this and I started...

"Me and Shahid, although are in a relationship but I don't love him. I still take him as a good friend and he knows this really well. Its just a tag that we are in a relationship but in real I really don't have feelings for him. We have never been on a date, a movie or even a single outing. We hardly have phone conversations too. So, its like for our friendship's sake I am with him and I will always be with him the way he wants me to be as I don't wanna loose him... he loves me a lot and I think one day I will fall in love with him... I wanted to clarify this to you because I think we can be good friends and good friends know each and every thing about each other."

He smiled at me and we shook hands. Then we hugged each other and went off back on our ways...

Three days passed and Shahid hadn't replied to any of my messages.

Not even a congrats SMS for my victory in the model competition.

I texted him in anger, "See if you don't wanna talk to me, you may say clearly. But don't behave like this."

He replied, "You wanted to break-off our relation na? You are free... you may go..."

I replied, "What are saying? Are you out of your mind?"

He didn't reply. I again texted –what is the matter honey? Please tell??

He called me up and said, "Anushree... and he started crying."

"What happened yaar??"

"Why did you did this to me??", he somehow managed to speak.

"What????", I replied as I was shocked and really had no idea of what was going on.

"See... I trusted you a lot. I loved you a lot. I never thought that you will ditch me like this??"

I was wondering why was he saying all this and he continued "If you loved Kush and not me, then you should have told this clearly na??? I would have left you... but why you..."

And I interrupted, "What the hell are you saying Shahid? I never ditched you?"

"I saw you hugging Kush and saying that you don't love me that day when you won that model prize .. I came there to be with you during your result out times, had brought flowers for you but... scene was entirely different... I hate you Anushree... never ever try to call me back. I will never forgive you. I really hate you. You will never be able to be happy in your life. I curse you..." and he disconnected the call.

What was this???

I was all in tears. He left me. I never ditched him.

Whatever he saw was true but whatever he heard was incomplete.

I know it was my fault. I mean I had no right to accept anyone's proposal when I didn't have feelings for him. It was a pure betrayal. But during the time, I was loyal to him. I never every lied to him. I wanted to tell him everything but he was busy so we couldn't talk much.

I still can't believe that he cursed me... how can a person curse a person whom he loves truly...

I tried to talk to him, made so many phone calls and left messages but not a single try of mine was responded...

I realized it was all over so I decided not to get back to him. I know it would hurt him even more if I go back to him. The Chapter was closed and so I let that be the way it was...

As time passed, Kush became an important part of my life. I realised that he was the guy who helped me and cared for me throughout and never expected anything in return.

We use to chit chat and do messaging all the day and till the late night. We shared each and every moment of our lives. I don't know when he started living in the illusion that I was in love with him. This thing was revealed when once during the month of January, I told him about my crush on a guy who was one year junior to me.

Actually he wasn't my crush, I liked him because of his looks and hardly knew him but once during my conversation with Kush, I said it just like that. He became furious and started shouting on me as if I was his girlfriend.

I don't understand this mentality of boys. I mean if a girl is talking and chatting with you all day and over nights, sharing things with you then automatically she is declared as your girlfriend. What the heck is this.

And in my out-of-this-world case, a girl named Tashi Ahuja, played a very special role.

She was Kush's sister and my junior. A girl with extra-ordinary mind. She had a special power to judge the difference between the love *waali* feeling and the friendship *waali* feeling!!

And so, Miss Tashi Ahuja was convincing Mr. Kush Ahuja from the day of my break-up with Shahid, that I did that break up because of Kush. I had fallen for Kush but as I am very much scared of him, so I was unable to express my feelings to him. And yes, one thing more- Kush should not propose me again because if he did so I out of my shy nature, might break up with him too and leave him forever. And the best part was, Kush was very much and very deeply convinced with this bullshit story of Tashi Ahuja and so he behaved with me according to this scenario only.

After Kush told me this wonderful story, I was speechless. I mean how can a person be so dumb in love.

Atleast once, he should have confirmed. By that time, I understood nothing was selfless, neither his care nor his concern.

It was just because he had an illusion that I loved him too.

So, by the end of my schooling, my life was a full mess.

I had a fight with Tashi for ruining my friendship with Kush and filling Kush's mind with all that bullshit and imaginary stuff of hers.

Kush had totally turned out into a typical villain. He took an oath that he would not let me marry any other guy... he also warned me to stay away from all the guys of this whole world.

Kriti, who was actually a best friend of mine, also choose Kush's friendship over mine as she found that choosing his side was more correct than mine as according to her I was a very bad girl who had no respect for true feelings and had ditched two guys till now who loved me more than their lives.

So last day of my school was almost same as the first day of my school. I was all alone, just one difference was that on the first day I was willing to make friends and make memories. And on the last day, I didn't even want to turn back and look at any of them.

My mind was asking a question to my heart. What kind of people are these? If they really cared for me or had even an inch of concern, then just once, at least once, they would have tried to listen to me and believe what I felt and what I wanted to say? But all through this scene, I was just a numb part who on one side was being shown people who loved and cared for me a lot and on the other side there was nobody who heard what I wanted to say and nobody tried to trust me...

With a question "what exactly was my fault?" I decided to leave Delhi and move back to Kanpur with my family.

Kanpur was my home town and a city I am in love with. It gained more importance over Delhi especially because Delhi made me experience such horrible days of my life.

I didn't want to be in touch with any of my DAVian friends and so I changed my number and didn't inform anyone about me going back to Kanpur.

With the good set of experience of being misunderstood, betrayed by best friends, class politics and all that, I joined Bachelor of Business Administration (BBA) in CSJMU, Kanpur.

I had by that time firmly decided that I would not trust anyone, would not expect anyone to be a good friend of mine, no crush -love jokes and *tafris,* and would stay away from all those people whom I came to know whether they like or love me, no matter how much important they are for me.

The time of entrance exam in CSJMU and the day of commencement of the semester have a difference of two months. I was all free during that month of July, year 2007.

That time, orkut.com had a great boom. Everybody was crazy about this new social networking site.

I made an account in that too. As it had options to join communities, I too joined many. The list of my joined communities reached the number of 450 which include communities like I love Shahrukh Khan, I love Shahid Kapoor, I love rains, Dancers Zone, Singing is my passion, Paulo Coelho, and so on... I also joined my old school's community which was *Dr. Virendra Swarup Public School, Civil Lines.* Although it was just a small decision of joining a community with no other thoughts in mind, till date for me this was the best decision I have ever made.

I got in touch with all the childhood friends of mine. We chatted lots about my school changing and shifting to Delhi. To my amazement, I found that all the friends still remember me. They all asked me the same question as to *why you left the school and without even informing any of us...??? we were worried and we actually missed you a lot.*

This was the best day of my life. Especially when I had such wonderful experiences of friends in Delhi ...

Scarcasm

Getting back my childhood friends was like getting back my life...

In a month, before the commencement of my semester and start of my college life, I was back to normal, just as previously I was–happy and cheerful. And all the credit goes to my childhood friends who didn't change in this span of six years, who remembered me and missed me all through. . .

First day in college was quite embarrassing. I got ragged from my seniors although ragging wasn't allowed but still, we juniors cannot complain because ragging is a part of college life and is of equal importance in building up one's confidence level.

P.S. this was told to us by our seniors : P

I told my hobby as singing and reading books during my intro-session, so first I was told to sing a song for which I sang "*Aapki nazaro ne samjha...*" and after that I was being told to tell a fairytale in front of the whole class, a big bunch of seniors and super-seniors too.

Now this was actually very embarrassing as I had to narrate a fairy-tale. Out of my nervousness I narrated *Jack and the bean-stalk* !!

After the completion of my story, everybody was like "Awww, such a cute girl she is..." "Oh wow... what a nice story" and all that. Some actually praised and others just made fun of me.

With all the memories of my school life in my heart, I promised to myself to not to trust anyone and not to get involved in anyone's personal matter.

Miss destiny already had decided something for me.

First year of BBA was really good. Made new friends. Tried to come out of the bad memories of my school life and also from that fear in my heart that I might get misunderstood again in front of anyone and then had to face a big problem. Most of the times I was busy in chatting with my Old school childhood friends.

First year passed as if it was of a moment...

In Second year, we were the seniors.

*Spandan,* My university's youth annual festival was about to happen. I never thought this youth fest would actually change my thoughts, feelings and life up to this extent.

It was the month of Feb. and we all were busy in the preparation of our performances. Me and my friends had prepared for the group dance. We practiced a lot before the auditions. One of my friends ran coaching classes near our college, so he hired and decided that place for our group dance practices. We used to have fun during our practices.

Till date, those two weeks of practice sessions of our group dance were the best days during my college life. We used to practice extra-time on Saturdays and Sundays. One of our senior Sirs named Vicky, was the main lead who choreographed our dance. He was actually a very awesome dancer. He had won many prizes and also had participated in many TV dance shows. We all were very confident that this year also we would win the prize as Vicky sir was with us to guide us. He took me as his partner along with eight friends of mine.

As its quite usual to have people in the same class who are quite envious and jealous, we also had a rival group. Actually at first they were very friendly with us and they proposed us to keep them in our group. But as our group was already over-crowded with eight side dances with one lead pair, we denied to keep them in our group. So just to take revenge from us, they made a new group of six people and stepped on the dance floor as our rivals.

A day before our group dance auditions was the audition of singing competition. One of a very dear friend named Sudeep participated in the singing competition. As it was the matter of our department and also he was a good friend of ours, we went to cheer and support him up during his final round of auditions.

It was 10:30 a.m. and Sudeep was rehearsing for his song which he sang in the auditions. He chose –*Mere naina, sawan bhadho,* an oldie by Kishore Kumar ji.

After he rehearsed finally I quoted – "No matter how many people would participate, you are going to win for sure!!!"

Sudeep laughed and replied - "Oyeee you are wrong! You haven't heard Arnav yet!!"

I exclaimed – "Arnav???????"

He said – "Yes!! Arnav!! He is the best and I am damn sure he is going to win for sure."

I replied in a haughty tone - "Now who is Arnav??"

"He is a B.tech 2nd year mechanical student!!" –said Sudeep with pride as if he was his best friend.

"Shameless creature!! Being from the BBA Deptt. You are promoting a guy of B.tech. Not fair!!"–I Joked and we all laughed.

"Well, jokes apart!! You surely must listen to him dear. I am sure, you yourself will start praising him", Sudeep interrupted.

I said – "Its impossible!!"

"Okay!! Its already 11. Final round for the auditions is just about to start, come along and listen to him and then decide. And yes one thing more??? Especially for you Anushree", replied Sudeep.

"What???" –I exclaimed.

"He is also a Kishore Kumar songs and ghazals fanatic, and mostly sings songs of this genre only. Just like you! I am sure.. you'll like him!!" –he told.

By ending of this conversation, we five friends went inside the auditorium.

With a cloud-high attitude, I asked Sudeep – "Where is he?"

He made a weird face as if he has forgotten our conversation about Arnav. He asked – "Who???"

"Arey the one you were praising few minutes before!!" –I replied.

"Oh Arnav!! He isn't here yet", said Sudeep and went off for his turn.

We all started hooting for Sudeep. On listening to the loud cheers for Sudeep, it seemed that Sudeep had the highest number of supporters.

Sudeep's performance was really appreciable.

After his performance, the anchor announced – "And the next participant is Arnav Gupta of B.Tech second year."

And entered Arnav from the side door of the auditorium with his group of 20-25 boys just like a V.I.P.

He looked damn confident although his looks weren't that much appealing as I had imagined singers to have. He was a simple looking short- heighted boy with a fair complexion.

With his entry, the students there in the auditorium started hooting the double as in that of Sudeep's turn.

He really seemed like a celebrity that time. Girls sitting at the back of my seat screamed 'All the best Arnav! You are the best'.

My Geez!! He is a rockstar or something –I wondered.

It literally took ten minutes to calm down the crowd inside the audi. I was wondering if he is actually that famous, then how hadn't I come across him since last two years.

A friend of mine named Aparna told me that he was last year's singing competition champ. She also reminded me how I came late to the college that day and missed hers and Arnav's performance. She bagged the second position last year. I wonder, why wasn't she participating that year. Well, anyways so coming back to Mr. Popular i.e. Arnav.

He started his song with an *Alaap* which was actually very mesmerizing. When all people were hooting I was totally lost in it. The attitude full face of mine was switched to the jaws down smiling one.

Then he started with the song. It was a ghazal *Kisi nazar ko tera intezar aaj bhi hai* from the movie *Aitbaar*.

My Souls!! This was one of my favorites. I mean I just loved this song. He sang so well, that during all his performance I was just smiling and looking at him. His voice went deep within me and touched so much that I actually got goose-bumps after hearing the first stanza.

I was just so wrong. He is an awesome singer and has no comparison with anyone here.

I was so lost in his performance that I couldn't listen to what my friends were saying. His performance ended and the audi echoed with the sound of 'once more - once more' for his song. When on the one hand all the people there were clapping for him, I was just gazing towards him and was actually feeling glad that I heard him. The anchor requested all to maintain silence and let them proceed towards the auditions of the participants left and also promised that Arnav would sing twice in the final performance of his and so the mob was calmed down. After finishing his performance he again went off with his friends leaving behind his new admirer which was ME!!

The next day was the day of my group dance auditions!

That day, destiny and luck wasn't in our favor I guess.

When on one side, I wanted Arnav to see my dance and notice me, on the other side I wanted to give my best today to get through auditions. Neither of these two happened!!!

We performed our level best but were unable to clear even the first round of the auditions. This was actually a big insult for Vicky sir and even to me.

And the rival group cleared all the rounds and also was short listed amongst the groups in final round.

I cried a lot on hearing the results. I was feeling guilty as I thought I was distracted from the dancing and my concentration was on finding Arnav in the crowd of the people who were there in the auditorium... but many a people came to us telling that me and Vicky sir were fab. Fault was of the other group members. Synchronisation is the most important element on the group dance and that was missing from our group and so we lose.

This was the first time ever that I or Vicky Sir were rejected in a dance audition. Dance was our passion. So, we decided to prove ourselves. I thought of not thinking about Mr. popular again and with this firm decision, we (I and Vicky Sir) took part in solo dancing competition.

Either luck was in our favor or we really danced well on the final day of our performance. But results were totally surprising. In group dance, my rival group came second. And in the solo dance competition, Vicky Sir came first and I was awarded with the special award which was introduced that year only. The award of *Spark of the event*. This was a real surprise for me and my friends even for my Deptt. As I used to be very reserved in nature, hardly told anyone about my likes and dislikes, people who knew me and saw me were totally astonished. I was happy as I proved myself on the dance floor.

But on the other hand, I missed Arnav's final performance again as I had to attend another Science Quiz event in which I had participated. I was very disappointed with this.

The next day after the prize distribution, when I was sitting with my friends in the Nescafe coffee corner inside my campus, I received a text message on my mobile.

It was from an unknown number which said - Congratulations Miss Anushree!!!

I replied -Thanks a lot. Who's this??

He replied -Your well-wisher! And since yesterday, your fan!!

I -Name pls?

Unknown No.-Sorry I can't tell my name right now but trust me I won't disturb or harass you!!

I -Please don't text me again, ever!!!!

As he wasn't telling his name, so I saved his number as 'Rains'.

Rains -sorry I can't sustain this order of yours. I would text you daily but yes I would never ever force you to reply.

After reading this SMS, I decided not to reply him any more. Six months thereafter, I still got his messages daily. Messages were usually like :-

- You looked really good today.

- Color purple suits you a lot.

- I am your first fan, so please try to value me : P

- Came to know that you scored 2nd topper position, congrats sweety.

- You look awesome when you smile.

And so on...

This was getting so annoying that I started feeling guilt for him. He knows that I read his messages daily, I am aware that he is always around me in the college and I know his feelings for me too... and then too I don't respond, not even for a single message. I am not that rude, neither I am that cruel. So I decided to talk to him for the last time, try to make him spit out his name and if this doesn't work, I would change my number!!

I texted him –why are you doing all this? Please tell who are you?

Rains replied –I knew that you would reply one day. My wait is finally over. Thank u so much.

I –No please. You getting me wrong. Please tell your name?

Rains –I'm sorry I can't. Not right now. But would come in front of you very soon and be your friend before you leave this college.

I was thinking what to reply meanwhile again he texted me –There is a request from you?

I replied –What?

Rains –Its my birthday tomorrow, 16 Sept. I want you to wish me. Will you...???

I thought for a while then I decided not to reply him again and would change my number the next day.

Next day on 16 Sept. when I was just about to change the sim card, I thought of wishing him. I texted him –Happy birthday!

He replied –thank you so so sooooo soooooo much for wishing. I was desperately waiting for your SMS. Thanks a lot that you wished me. It really means a lot.

After reading this SMS, I switched off my phone, took out the sim card and changed it to a new one.

With the change of sim card, all this annoying sequence ended and soon started a new phase.

But despite the fact that one year had passed, Arnav's performance in Spandan, was still fresh in my mind. All the year, me and my friends who knew that I was actually having a crush on Arnav, tried to talk to him. we made so many plans but all in vain. Neither of us had those much guts, that we would approach a guy for friendship. I searched him on Orkut but didn't find him.

My friends used to say that I had fallen for him as crush lasts only for few months and my craze seemed never ending. I used to look at him hiding from the side of the pillars, used to sit near his table in the cafeteria and so on. I actually behaved like a secret admirer for him.

A year passed... I was a 'super senior' now. A term used by students to refer to third year students in my college.

As this was my final year and still my craze for Arnav wasn't gone, me and my friends made a superb plan. The plan was that this year I would also be participating in the singing competition as it was by default for Arnav to participate. And so, we can easily talk with each other during the practices as it always happened that people became friends during the fests.

So, this year along with dancing, I was also now a singing participant.

The day when first round of auditions were going to take place, I saw Arnav. He was wearing a white shirt and blue denims. I was so scared to talk to him that many times before my singing competition registration, I decided to back-off. I was wondering he is a damn good singer seems as if he is trained in singing and I a normal one. Thought he would laugh after listening to my song. But all my friends forced and insisted me to move ahead and participate. A friend of mine named Srisha, who knew about Arnav was also participating in the same competition. Srisha was a very different girl. A full-on cartoon and a huge fan of Smurfs. When I used to say 'Oh Geez!!', others used to say 'Oh My God' 'Oh my goodness' etc., she used to say 'Oh My Smurfs'. Isn't it funny. Her voice sounded like a Donald duck and so we called her Donald. I, Donald and Haya were the best of friends that time. Our trio always rocked although we three were very different in nature, Donald was highly extrovert and loud. I was a kind-of shy and introvert and Haya was soft spoken yet high tempered.

So when we saw Arnav entering the Audi, Donald decided to talk to Arnav. And to her guts, she went to talk to him. They talked for five minutes and then she came back with a smile.

"Oh my Smurf!! He is sooooo sweet just like a smurf!!" -said Donald in excitement.

I was completely indulged into blushing that time.

Haya asked – "What did you both talk???"

"Well, I asked him that which song was he singing this year???" -replied Donald.

"And?????" -I inquired in curiosity.

"And...!!! There is a surprise for you all...!!" -said Donald.

"What surprise??" –asked Haya.

"Well, he is the event coordinator this year and so he isn't participating nor singing."

I was so happy to hear this. I exclaimed – "Really??"

"Yesss!! This is a good news!!" –said Haya.

Our so-exciting conversation was interrupted by Arnav on the stage announcing the names of the participants. I heard my name from him for the first time and it sounded really different as if it was new to me.

I was just smiling and blushing. My friends said that I was totally gone for Arnav because I was smiling for no reason. May be, he was my first crush till now that is why I was feeling like this but whatever it was... it was truly beautiful!!

And soon auditions started.

Before my turn, somebody said "Where is Anushree Sharma of BBA?"

I said – "Yeah!! its me.."

The guy said – "Come in front."

I replied 'okay' and started heading towards the stage. I wasn't aware as to why I was being called. I was standing at the side of the stage. I tried to find out where Arnav was. When I saw him, my goodness!! He was already looking at me. We had an eye contact for the first time and I out of my shyness ignored looking there and started looking somewhere else. But within a second I realized that he was trying to say something. I looked at him again, and he said 'you are next' in a sign language with a combination of lip-sing.

I smiled and nodded my head to yes.

Oh Geez!! He talked to me!! he noticed me!! after a few moments I again looked at him and he was looking at me. We passed smiles to each other for the first time. It was just me and him. I felt as if the whole crowd vanished for few seconds. It was really a beautiful feeling.

Now on my turn, as I was mesmerized by the incident which happened few minutes back, I thought I couldn't sing now. I was damn nervous. I reached the centre of the stage as the whole crowd started hooting. I tried to find where my friends were sitting but all in vain. The jury faculty said "Start!!" and I went blank. I closed my eyes for a second. Opened thereafter and saw Arnav standing just next to the jury and judges. He smiled and wished 'all the best'. This all the best of his gave a true strength to me. I was about to sing *aapki nazro ne samjha* but I sang *Tu is tarah se meri zindagi mein shaamil hai* !! as it's a *ghazal*, so after every line of this song everybody shouted '*waah waah*' !! but as I was so nervous, I could feel that my voice was shivering.

According to me my performance was very bad and nobody on earth would select me because of this performance. After my performance, all people there clapped but Arnav was busy in writing something which actually disappointed me. I felt like he found mine boring and so he didn't hear the whole song. On the other hand, Donald's performance was very nice and we were sure that she will pass through this round.

While all my friends were appreciating my song, I was sitting with my sad face on the stair-case of the building.

Meanwhile Haya came in running. She told that results would be declared within an hour.

After an hour, we went to see the list of people promoted to the second round. To our surprise, Donald's name wasn't there but mine was there!!

What???? Was I really selected and Donald rejected??? There might be a mistake, I thought!!

I decided to talk about my friend to that coordinator, who so ever it may be. This was a clear mistake, I didn't sing well then too I was selected and Donald who sang really well, got rejected.

The next day morning, I and Haya went to the auditorium at 9:30. Round 2 of the auditions was to start from 10 a.m.

Arnav, with his group of five were sitting there with the list of participants.

We went near them and Haya said - "Excuse me!!"

He looked at us and said - "Ohh! Anushree... you? Say??"

Now this was really unexpected. I mean if Haya was talking then he should have replied to Haya but rather he said to me. But then too, I decided to remain silent. I just smiled and Haya began - "I think there is problem with the list of selectees."

"What? I didn't get you?" -replied Arnav.

I said - "See, I sang terrible yesterday and then too my name is there on the list and my friend Srisha Verma hasn't got selected although she sang so well? She deserves to be in the round 2".

Arnav smiled and said - "Well Anushree, this is your illusion that you sang terrible because you really sang beautiful. Your voice is really good. So you too deserve to be in the next round. And if its about your friend, then don't worry I will include her name too."

And what??? He was convinced to write Donald's name??? So easily??? Without much of insisting!! And the main thing is that he noticed me? He appreciated my singing and my voice too!! I felt this was the best day till now.

After a wait of an year, finally we started talking.

I replied with a 100 watt smile – "Really? Thanks a lot!!"

"By the way, I am Arnav and you????" –Arnav said offering a hand-shake to Haya.

Haya replied – "I am Haya."

Then he looked at me and said – "You really have a good choice of songs. Ghazal that you sang yesterday was my favourite!!"

"Thanks..." –I replied trying to manage not to blush.

"No No! don't say thanks..." –said Arnav, meanwhile his friend interrupted.

"And Hi, I am Shikhar!!! Arnav's friend." –said he to me.

We shook hands very formally followed by my reply 'Pleasure' to him!!

This first formal meeting of we four soon turned into a good friendship. During the fest, we became good friends. We practiced for songs together and cleared rounds one by one.

As I also participated in the dance competition, I used to go for dance practices after the singing ones.

In between these audition and preparation days, my throat choked and for that reason I had to quit the singing competition. But as Donald was already in, I used to attend the practices. Every time after the practice session, Arnav used to sing a song on public demand. Sometimes a ghazal and sometimes a filmy song. But every time, it was a pleasure to hear him.

Luckily I won the solo dance competition that year. He came to me and said 'congrats' for the results. That day we talked for full one hour sitting at the backside of the audi, all alone.

We shared our experiences of this fest. As it was the last night of the event, he told how much relaxed he was for the successful happening of the event. He also told me that he wasn't expecting much from my dancing but he was very surprised to see my dancing.

It was like a fairy tale. Me and Arnav were sitting all alone, backside of the audi. We could see the visible stalls of food and people enjoying the food. It was night 8:30. Cool breeze was blowing. But nobody was there to disturb me. I was so busy in that moment that I didn't even know where my friends were.

If god would have granted one wish that time, I would have asked him to pause that moment.

He was holding his bike's key-ring which had a Arnav engraved on the metallic plate. I took that key-ring in my hands and said – "Really nice key-ring!!"

He replied – "Thanks... you may keep it if you want!!"

I laughed and said – "Nooo... its your name written over it. How can I keep it??"

He smiled and replied – "Hmmm!!"

Meanwhile his phone rang. It was Shikhar's call!! He wanted to meet Arnav immediately because of some problem which occurred back-stage. Arnav told me and left. He was in so much of hurry that he left his key-ring with me only. After he was gone I saw his key-ring in my hands. Till that time, we haven't exchanged our numbers. Haya had!! I called Haya up and asked for Arnav's number.

This was my first call to Arnav!! I wouldn't have called by myself to him if it wasn't this urgent. But I had to return his key-ring.

He picked up the call and said – "Hello??"

I said – "Hi.. you left your key-ring with me Arnav!!"

He replied – "Ummm Who's this???"

"Ohh!! Its me Anushree.!!" –I replied.

"Ohh I am sorry. Where are you?" – he asked.

I told him that I was near the entrance of the auditorium. He came there to take his key-ring from me. He smiled and said 'sorry' for leaving his key-ring with me.

We both went off. My friends were teasing and asking me the whole story. I we were sitting, what all did we talk about and how he left his key-ring with me!!

Meanwhile my phone rang. It was Arnav!!

I picked up in curiosity and said – "Hello!!"

"Ummm Anushree??" -he said.

"Yeah!! Arnav???" -I replied pretending as if I haven't saved his number and am trying to memorize his voice!

"Yeah!! Well, wanted to ask. Is this your number???" -he inquired.

I replied - "Yes!! Why?"

"No!! just like that... ok then. Bye!! Good night!!" and he disconnected the call after saying this.

Conversation was strange but this was sure that he was also interested in our friendship growing more stronger.

That night only he texted me a good night forwarded SMS.

With this really interesting start of our friendship, we as time passed became really good friends.

We used to meet during our lunch hour. We chatted through messages whole day till we fell asleep at night. Soon our night message chats turned into night calls. He used to call me every alternate night after 11. Then we used to talk for two to four hours discussing all things about college, studies, movies, aim and family. We shared our childhood memories with each other. We used to set the same channel on TV and watched the same program together. Passing comments and teasing each other soon became our habits. As both of us had same choice of songs, we enjoyed watching *Sa re ga ma pa* on Zee TV at night in our unique way of watching together.

He told me about his dreams of being a singer...

I used to request him that one day when he will become a big singer, to make me meet Shahrukh Khan. He use to laugh hearing this and say - "Ok for sure!!"

Our bond grew stronger and stronger and soon he became an important part of my life. He also told me that he counts me in his list of best-friends. I was happy wondering that I was important to him. His friend Shikhar also took my number and Arnav took Haya's.

Now we were a group of four people –Me, Haya, Arnav and Shikhar.

It felt complete and seemed perfect when we were together.

Once on a phone call he demanded to hear a song from me and I kept a condition that I'll only sing if he would sing after my song. He agreed to this. I sang *Lag ja galey ke phir hasi raat ho na ho.* After listening to my song, he went silent for some time. I asked what happened twice thrice then he said – "I have never heard something so beautiful ever before".

This comment of his made me blank. Then after few seconds of silence, I replied – "Now your turn!!"

And he sang *Din dhal jaye haaye, raat na jaaye* which truly was magical. It was just he singing and me listening moment.

This was happening for the first time that I heard somebody singing on phone and I sang for somebody. And most importantly that somebody was my one year old college crush Arnav!! This was truly unbelievable.

*'Magic does happens and Wishes Do come true!!'* By now, I had started believing on this phrase.

Our friendship grew so stronger with time that we started sharing each and every moment of our day. From Good Morning to Good Night, we were all the time connected. I had started trusting him.

On the other hand, Shikhar and I had also become good friends. We used to chat online for hours and hours. Shikhar was funny guy and so he often used to crack jokes and tease me for Arnav.

One day, during my online chat with Shikhar I came to know that Arnav was engaged with a girl who lives in Dehradun. He is a big time flirt and his next target is me. He said will use and throw me. I wasn't believing his words so he told me to ask Haya as Haya was my best friend and she would never ever lie to me.

The most surprising thing for me was that Haya too said the same things as Shikhar. Now this was unbelievable but as I trusted Haya a lot, I made her believe me that there was nothing wrong between me and Arnav, no affair was there. We were just best of friends and that crush kind of feeling was gone from my heart.

This was truly unexpected.

I went to *Ganga Bairaj* all alone... to escape the world. Many of my friends by now knew that I had a crush on Arnav. It was hard to face them. I was feeling as if my life has ended and I would never be able to live a happy life, I would never be able to trust anyone... I would never be able to love anyone. I cried my heart out...

One moment I felt like jumping over the bridge and killing myself... it was my first crush... or you can say, my first love... I had dreamt of living and leading whole life with him... I had dreamt of a married life with him... and all dreams were shattered in just one hiccup.

I felt like calling Arnav and asking him ... asking him why he did that? If he was already committed, then why did he start getting too much involved with me... why he cares for me.. why he shared his utmost personal family problems with me... when he had that someone special in his life, then why did he make me feel like the special one in his life... I was innocent, I was living my life happily... if he wouldn't have entered my life then I would have forgotten him with time like a sweet dream...

Who on earth gave him the right to play with my emotions...

But I didn't do anything... I just cried my heart out... I cried for myself... and I cried for him...

My phone was continuously ringing. It was Shikhar...

Finally after three hours, I picked up his call when I was back to my senses. He seemed really worried. He asked my location and told me to wait for him there only...

Shikhar reached after half an hour. I was still there sitting in despair.

He tried to console me... starting with his philosophical lecture on love, life, trust and relationships... he suddenly jumped over to his stupid PJs which made me laugh...

He promised me that he and Haya will always be there with me and would never ever leave me...

Few weeks passed.

Now Shikhar was someone different to me, he was a best friend, a guide, trustworthy guy for me with whom I could share all my problems. I also told her that if there was something in his life then he would for sure have told me as he had said that I was important to him and he liked sharing things with me.

It was really hard to believe what Shikhar and Haya said as both were each one of us' best friends, but Haya convinced me that she was right.

I promised to break my friendship with Arnav as Arnav had broken my trust in him. I thought I really knew everything about him but he forged me. He kept his relationship with that Dehradun girl hidden from me. If he really would have taken me as his true friend then he would have told about his relationship. But he didn't...

I started avoiding his phone calls. And slowly stopped replying to his messages...

Shikhar, during this time became a good friend. We started talking on messages. Every time we talked I used to ask him about Arnav as now me and Arnav were not in contact any more. He used to get angry whenever I mentioned Arnav's name as he said that Arnav doesn't deserve to be remembered by me as he had broken my trust. I should forget him. He is busy in his life and all that.

But my purpose of talking to Shikhar was that he was Arnav's friend although I used to take him as a good friend but he was more like Arnav's friend to me than my friend.

The month before my completion of BBA, Shikhar proposed to me. He said that he had fallen for me. He tried to convince me by saying that he tells each and everything to me, haven't kept anything hidden from me, would never break my trust etc.

He also confessed that an year before, the guy who used to send Text Message to me, who used to say that he was my well-wisher was actually Shikhar only. He told that he had fallen for me from the day he saw me performing on the stage last year and since then he was following me.

Now this was actually shocking.

As it was clear that I didn't have feelings for him and previously I already had done a mistake of saying yes to

Shahid although I didn't have feeling of love for him. So I decided to say no and I firmly rejected to his proposal. I told him that he was more like Arnav's friend to me than of my own. I gave him an option for us to remain good friends as we were because I really didn't want to lose such a good friend but he didn't agree for that. He opted to move away from my life...

That was really a tough phase for me. Now the only college friend I had was Haya, and even she stopped talking to me suddenly. I asked her for the explanation for doing so but she remained silent.

The last month was really hard for me. I had a good company of classmates but had lost my best buddies. Everybody use to ask me why me, Haya, Arnav or Shikhar are not talking to each other as it was visible to all that we had formed a group and we were happy being together always.

Where and what was my fault?

I trusted Arnav, was this my fault? Or I expected Haya that she would be always there for me? or I took Shikhar as a new sunshine buddy in my life?

If god would have granted one wish that time, I would have asked to give answer to all my questions.

This was the second time in my life that I had faced a betrayal from my only best friend. Previously it was Kriti and Now Haya!!

With the ending for BBA, I promised myself not to trust anyone again in life. Neither as friend or best friend nor as love.

I only had handful of childhood buddies with whom I never shared these incidents of my life. We used to talk nonsense all the time and this actually worked as a stress-buster for me.

I decided to move on and promised myself that I would not trust anyone again, ever.

To move on and to try my luck in the field of Journalism and Mass Communication, I joined Amity University in Lucknow with the hope of fresh start in life.

It was going to be an experience as hostel life hadn't been experienced by me before.

I decided to live in a private girls hostel than in a college hostel.

As Lucknow is just 100 kms (approx) from Kanpur, so I reached Lucknow and my hostel, a day before the commencement of my session.

I met Nisha -my roommate.

She was a B. Tech Second year student. With a simple 'Hi', we started our first conversation followed by a formal introduction. I was too shy to talk to new people, so couldn't interact with the other girls in PG that day. I reached hostel at 8 p.m. and went off to sleep at 9.

It was a tough night for me, as this was the first time that I was sleeping away from my mummy or family. All strangers were there around me and I knew I had to live with them now. I cried by myself silently and went off to sleep...

I was missing my home!!!

The next day I got up with my mummy's call. It was actually a wake up call 'cause mummy knew that I would not wake up if somebody didn't ask me to.

I got up and got ready at a very fast pace.

I reached college before time. I new friend of my mine named Sania Anand whom I met during the entrance exam had told me to wait as she was on the way to college. So I decided to wait for here near the staircase.

As I was sitting on the staircase, suddenly a boy who was passing by dropped all his documents, papers and his file along with his phone too. He started picking up his papers and documents and I helped him to pick up his mobile and its part. We both sat down together on the staircase.

He was busy in talking to himself and organizing the sheets.

"Oh no!! what have I done" –he said.

"Here's your phone!!" –I said handing over his phone and its parts to him.

For the first time I noticed him. He was cute. Fair – clean shaved – wearing frameless specs. But he didn't notice me and was busy in talking to himself. When I gave his mobile to him, then also he took it and started putting the battery, back panel and all that back in order.

He switched on his phone.

I asked him – "Is your phone fine??"

"Yeah!! Luckily!!" –he replied.

He looked at me, raised his right eye-brow, smiled and said – "You new here???"

"Yeah!"

"First day????" -He asked.

"Yep!!!"

"Which course???"

"MJMC"

He laughed and said - "Ohhhh you are my junior!!"

"Junior??? You too pursuing MJMC??" -I inquired.

"Nooo!! I am doing MBA!! But as this is my final year, I am senior to you!!" -He giggled.

"Ohh okay" -I replied.

"So??"

"So??"

Meanwhile I heard Sania's voice coming from the back. We turned around and saw Sania coming.

I said - "She is my friend Sania!! I was waiting for her only".

"Ohh!! Okay. It was nice meeting you miss fresher!!" -He said.

I smiled and replied - "Same here!!"

"Ohh by the way, welcome to Amity miss!!" -he said and we both shook hands.

And he went away!!

Sania came running near me and asked - "Who was he??? Your boyfriend???"

"Oh no!! we just met ten mintues before!!" and I narrated the whole incident to her.

"What was his name??" –inquired Sania.

"I don't know... I forgot to ask!! But he is of MBA!!" –I replied.

"Ohh noooooo, he was sooooo cute. You missed the shot baby!!" –Sania said in a flirty tone.

"Leave yaar!! I am not interested....."

First day in college was quite good as I met new people from all different places. But I couldn't take off my mind from that boy. He was so appealing and attractive. Just like any bollywood star.

'But not again!! No more crush stories Anushree!!' I reminded myself and decided not to think of him any more. Class-mates of mine were good as I had already decided not to expect anyone to be my good friend here. I kept myself busy in reading novel most of the time.

Once in the library, I again met that MBA guy. He was standing in the queue next to me for issuing his book. He said – "Hey".

I looked at him and pretended as If I didn't recognize him.

I replied – "Sorry??"

He said – "Wait...!!" as it was his turn for giving the books to be issued.

We got our books issued. I was collecting my bag from the counter. He again came near me.

He said – "Girl, your first day in college You met a guy who helped you and you forgot that guy?"

I replied – "Oh yeah... MBA second year right???"

"Bingo!!!" –he replied with excitement.

"So Miss fresher, How are you??" –He asked.

"I am good Mr. Senior!!" –I replied.

He laughed at this statement of mine and said – "You really have a good sense!!! I like you!!"

"Ohkay got to go!! Getting late for class!! See ya!!" – I said and started walking away!

Meanwhile he shouted 'Excuse me!!' from my back.

I turned back and asked "What???"

"I didn't catch your name????"

"Ohh!! I am Anushree!!"

"Pleasure meeting you Anushree, I am Samrat!" –said he.

This first meeting of ours turned into a good friendship as the months passed.

We had became good friends but my class-fellows out of their narrow-mindedness and cheap thoughts, assumed that we were in a relationship. They spread the news across the department that I was now committed to Samrat. When this shit news reached me I got very angry. It was high time now. In school, I had tags on me that I was Kush's girlfriend then of Shahid. In BBA, I was tagged as Arnav's girlfriend and then of Shikhar's. And now, Samrat's !!

What the heck was going on in my life. Either it was unlucky for me to make boys as good friends or it was my mistake to be so much frank and friendly to boys which people misunderstood and forced them to think that I was in a relationship.

But the thing with me was that being an introvert in nature, I barely was friends with many. And with those who I befriended, I got extremely close and attached to them as I liked spending time with them and sharing things, may it be a boy or a girl. And by that time I realised that this was my biggest mistake. Till date, although we say we are modern or uptodate but still we possess a narrow-mind within ourselves which forces us to take things in a wrong way. If a boy and a girl are seen together alone, then it is by default understood that they are in a relationship.

In short, Perception was similar as that of Salman's movie *Maine Pyar Kiya*, which said –'*ek ladka aur ladki kabhi dost nahin ho sakte!!!*" and people firmly follow this.

This time I decided not to own any tag upon me, so once in a class I told all my class-mates that I was single and genuinely least interested in having a relationship with anyone, neither I had one. I broke my friendship with Samrat. Although I had a sad feeling within me of loosing my only good friend in Amity but this time I chose to be alone rather than earning a wrong image just for sake of this new three months old friendship.

Even after I stopped talking to Samrat, mine and his mutual friend named Zaid, who was in my class only continued to spread rumors about me and Samrat. He cooked a story that me and Samrat are just showing-off that they aren't in contact, although they talk a lot when alone and avoid talking with each other in front of the crowd.

Two semesters passed!! Amity was getting more and more suffocating day by day. After joining Amity, the only good that happened to me was that my friendship with my childhood buddies was increased. From messaging, now we were promoted to phone-calls and long night non-sense chats. Whenever I felt home-sick, my childhood friends were always there to entertain me and to divert my mind from missing my home. Whenever I felt lonely or needed somebody by my side, I had these friends...

I always used to wonder that if I wouldn't have left the school in 2001 in class 7th, I would have maintained a much stronger bond with these friends. But no worries, not during these ten years but now I was having these friends of mine with me. Also, Tanshika the only person in my life, who was there with me all the time during all the phases.

I felt complete with their presence in my life.

After my summer vacation, it was the time for college to get re-opened for the commencement of the third semester.

I was already one week late to join. It was Monday and I caught 7 'o clock bus from Kanpur which reached Alambagh bus stand of Lucknow at 9:30. It almost takes an hour to reach my hostel from Alambagh.

I reached my room at 10:45. I was already late for my class. I called-up one of my classmates who usually used to go with me from my hostel to college but she already had reached college. I decided to go by auto-rickshaw as I didn't have any other option.

It was 11 and I was still waiting for auto at the stand.

Sometimes in life, things never come up when you need them the most as there is something else kept inside the bag for you.

There passed Zaid and Samrat in their bike.

I saw Samrat after a span of two months. He was looking at me. I couldn't make eye-contact with him as there was a guilt within me that I broke our friendship for sake of those stupid rumors. But actually, those stupid rumors mattered a lot for me because this wasn't the first time for me. Previously I had faced a lot of problems because of all this only.

Zaid stopped the bike and shouted my name and asked 'Where?'

I replied – "College!!"

"Come Along!! With us..." said Zaid.

Samrat was sitting head-down on Zaid.

I replied – "Noo!! Its okay. I'll come by auto."

Zaid insisted me to sit by saying – "Please don't waste time, we are already late for the class!!"

I was feeling damn restless and embarassed too. I asked – "Tripling??"

Zaid said "Yes !! of-course!! Now please come fast!!"

I agreed just because of two reasons:

No.1 – I was getting late for the class.

And No. 2 –I didn't have any other option as well.

I started struggling to sit on the bike without touching Samrat. Samrat without looking at me offered his hands to me so that I could hold them and take help of his hands to sit.

As we were getting late for the class, Zaid was riding as fast as he can. And I being a bike-phobic too, was getting scared but wasn't getting anything to hold. Samrat turned his face halfway and said – "Hold me!!"

And I immediately held him from the shoulders. Soon a flashback of happy times of ours started coming in front of my eyes. The times when we were friends. The times when we were happy.

Samrat was silent. We reached college. Samrat went off towards his department and I and Zaid towards ours.

We didn't even say a formal 'Bye' to each other and soon I realized that we weren't friends any more.

I was upset thinking all this. Meanwhile Zaid again didn't a *kaminapan*. He again spread his own cooked story that previously Anushree's and Samrat's break-up news was true. But meanwhile in the holiday, they patched up again!!

This was it!!

It was the time of September, and I was totally fed up of all things incidents happening in my life again and again!! God Why me!!!

What exactly is my fault!! I haven't lied to any one! I haven't murdered anyone not even committed a theft!! Why me? God!! Why me???

Enough of explaining truth in front of all. Enough of proving that I was always right and whatever happened wasn't my fault or whatever happened was due to a genuine reason.

It was my life but I felt like as if I wasn't having any right upon it. Other people were the owner of it and so they always assumed and cooked stories about it.

From that time, I decided not to explain anything to anyone as this was my life and I will live it in the way I want!! Not even a single entity on the earth would now make assumptions and decisions for my sake.

All through these times, some of my childhood buddies were there with me always...

I never shared all these incidents with them as I found it not worthy.

But for you, its less like sharing and more like a confession!!

Although, I had a crush on Arnav, no doubt it was deep one... but we were not more than friends... I was silly, I was stupid to behave filmy that time when I thought of killing myself for sake of my crush... I admit that I wasn't mature. But soon after a span of time I realized that it was my mistake to think that I was in love previously, although I wasn't... I never had been in love before... my past life was full of rumors and misconceptions about me, even if many a time I tried to clarify to many people, I wasn't successful in that.

I was an introvert. I was always misunderstood.

Nobody till date understood me as to what I wanted, what makes me happy or sad and why am I like this!!

So, now I would like to say sorry to god for making wrong decisions, to myself for not trusting my own-self and not listening to my heart but the other fake people and to all those people whom I have hurt unintentionally or intentionally...

Trust me, the only thing I had in my heart was the feeling and want of true friendship... Nothing else...

I hope, all will forgive me after listening to this story of mine...

# 9

# A Dream Came True

I was interrupted with the ringtone of my phone. It was 2:30 in the night and it was Vivaan's call.

I thought why is he calling at this time. Its too late. Is all fine? I worriedly picked up the phone –Vivaan??

He replied –'Hey sweetheart, really sorry to disturb you.'

I said –'What happened ? is everything alright?'

His voice sounded as if he was very happy. In an exciting tone he said –'Dear, I couldn't wait till the morning to let you know about...'

I said firmly –'About what Vivaan! Be clear..!!'

He replied –'I finished reading your *Before saying sorry* !! I just loved this book.'

"Really?" I replied making myself comfortable in my bed again "You scared me Vivaan... I thought something went wrong...!!"

"Noooo!!! Actually I was damn excited to tell this to you. So as soon as I finished this book I immediately called you up!" said he.

"You really liked it???" I asked again.

Actually it was quite difficult for me to believe that Vivaan was appreciating that book. If it was a fake appreciation then he wouldn't have called me up so late in the night. But still it was a bit hard to believe that he loved my first novel. And on the other side I was a bit scared too as he didn't doubt even for a single moment for my novel being a true story and not being a fictional work.

He replied –'Yes of-course!! Believe me girl, this novel is going to be amongst the best sellers of the country.'

"I don't hope for my novel to be listed amongst the best sellers, I just want all people to know what actually a girl faces when she is unable to express herself and on the contrary no one tries to understand her silence or gives her a chance to express herself." I replied.

"Really!! That girl in the novel really had a hard time during her school and college... but dear, I couldn't understand why have you written a Sorry Note in the end of this story?'" -asked Vivaan.

"Umm actually... leave Vivaan. It was just to gain more readers. For sake of an emotional dose !! Its just a trick!!" –I replied.

"Ohh!! But I loved it. But one more question?"

"Yeah???"

"I found this story incomplete!!" –said Vivaan.

Yes... this story was incomplete... it wasn't a story actually... It was my journey from 2001 till date. Now what should I have said!!

"It'll be completed one day Vivaan!!" –I replied.

"What?????"

"*Arrey*, leave!! I am glad that you liked the novel a lot. Lets go off to sleep now... I have to go on work tomorrow!!" –I said.

We wished 'Good Night' to each other and disconnected the call.

With the passing of weeks by weeks, my first novel started attaining popularity.

It became one of the most read novels of all times. Demand for my novel was increasing day by day. Soon, my publishers had the orders for the 3rd edition within 50 days of its release with the National Best Seller Tag on it.

Me and Vivaan were also living and continuing the beautiful relationship.

Once, I was going through my e-mails, rather should call the fan-mails I saw a mail from a very familiar e-mail address. On opening it, I saw it was of Kush's.

I was truly surprised to read it.

It said : 'Hey Anushree, I am so happy for you for your success. Please come back. I still love you a lot. We will never fight again. I am sorry that I misunderstood you. Please respond!!'

I decided not to respond, so I ignored it.

Some weeks later, I got a call from Kriti, my DAV school's bestie.

It was an unknown number, I had to receive it.

I said – "Hello??"

She said – "Awww my angel has become a writer!!"

"Who's this??" –I asked.

"Ohh, so you forgot my voice..???" –She replied.

"Please tell who you are??" –I said in an annoying tone.

"Your one and only best friend Anu, its me Kriti!!"

I was shocked to hear that it was Kriti. I wonder from where did she get my number? But I decided not to talk to her much.

I rudely said – "Thank you for calling my dear best friend, Please don't call on this number ever again!!!" and I disconnected the call.

She texted me after this which said –'How rude!! You have changed a lot. Now as you are a celebrity, you would not like to talk to a normal girl who once was your best friend.'

I felt like thrashing her on her face. Now that I am a famous writer, everybody has to come back. Everybody would take me as a very nice person and the time when I needed them the most, that time they all left me just like that without even thinking what would I feel.

I ignored that sms of hers.

It was November 23, when I got a call from my publishers who gave me a brilliant news. They told me that there is a Rising Writers Committee who every year appreciate the new and debutant authors with the best debutant author of the year. My publishers sent my name for the nominations. I got selected and this year, I was being given this award for my first novel *Before saying sorry*.

I was on the seventh heaven on hearing this news. It was really a great opportunity for me. It was a cause of true happiness as I was going to be awarded for my debut novel.

Soon, I was back to normal. I requested my publishers to ask that committee whether it is possible for them to make this event happen in my hometown, Kanpur?

They forwarded my request to that committee.

That committee agreed for this request as they got enough sponsors for that event.

Dates were finalized. It was for the next week. It was fixed on the 3rd of December.

Days were really getting hard to pass. I took leave for a week from office and reached Kanpur on 1st December.

2nd December night, that is yesterday, I was so happy and excited for next day's event that out of my excitement, I couldn't close my eyes and go off to sleep. Just was imagining what would be tomorrow's scenario. How things would happen...

# 10

# I Walked Away

Four hours to go for the award ceremony to be started.

I with my family members and Vivaan as well, were sitting together in the V.I.P. lounge in the banquet hall of Royal Cliff.

By this time, I had finally decided that I would not be telling any thing to Vivaan.

I was getting many congratulation calls from my friends and family. While I was busy in a call, a boy came in to Vivaan with a slip on which it was written "Anushree, please meet me outside the banquet hall".

That boy handed over that slip to Vivaan as he knew that he was my fiancée as I was busy on a call. Vivaan came to me with that slip. I was confused as to who might to the one to send that slip. I with Vivaan went out to find out who was that person.

To my amazement, it was Shahid. Yes! Shahid my school friend my first boyfriend whom I was never in love with. But what the hell was he doing here.

He came closer to me, hugged me and said – "Congrats Anu. I am really proud of you for your wonderful work in the novel. Please forgive me. I misunderstood you and left you."

He was so happy that he without any break was speaking continuously. I looked blank.

I said "Thanks!!"

He was astonished. He said – "Just thanks? We are meeting after such a long time and you said just a thanks? I should say thanks to you for writing that novel, else I would have been living in this illusion throughout my life that you broke my trust."

I interrupted him and said – "Wait Shahid!! First meet my fiancée Vivaan!!" and I introduced Vivaan to Shahid. Vivaan was really puzzled and I was scared.

Vivaan met Shahid in a very gentle way. They shook hands and greeted each other with a nice hello. Shahid looked really surprised and so was Vivaan.

Shahid asked me – "Fiancee?? You both are getting married?"

I replied – "Yes Shahid..."

Shahid gave me a fake smile and said – "I am really sorry Anushree!! Take care!"

And he left...

I told Vivaan that he was a classmate of mine in school when I was in Delhi.

I am sure this would puzzle anyone in this world and so was Vivaan.

He said – "You have a character named Shahid in your book who misunderstood the girl in the book??"

"Yeah... so?"

He said – "No.. I mean it was strange that he said sorry and all that. He behaved in a strange manner, unlike your other friends."

I nervously said – "Leave Vivaan. Lets go back!!"

Still two hours were left for my award distribution, there were some singing and dancing performances from the sponsor schools and dance academies going on.

Vivaan had to leave for Mumbai that night only after my award distribution. I was very nervous. Everybody was praising my work and my book but I deep within myself was very worried as I was praying to god not to give any twist or turn this day. But my fate never ever favors me, especially when I need it the most.

Vivaan went to talk to some invited friends of his.

I was sitting alone looking at the messages in my phone.

Suddenly my phone rang. It was a call from an unknown number. Series was of Kanpur only so I picked up thinking it would of a friend to congratulate me for my success.

Voice of a boy very known said- "Anushree?"

I replied – "Yes??"

"Can you please come to the second floor of this hotel? There is a lobby. I am waiting for you there."

This voice was actually giving my shivers as it was very known to me, I just was unable to recognize him. I replied – "Whose this???"

He replied – "Never thought that you'll forget my voice too..."

And he disconnected the call.

Now who might he be??

I ran towards the lift and reached straight to the second floor lobby.

I looked around but found no one.

Then I looked towards a guy who was standing with his face towards the wall looking at the painting on that wall.

I went near him and said – "Excuse me?"

He turned around.

It was Arnav!!!!!!!

What was he doing here? Really??? Arnav!!!!!!

I was completely shocked. Atleast he was least expected. In all the other cases, I was the culprit. I was being misunderstood so people came in apologizing. But in Arnav's case, he ditched me... he broke my trust although we were just good friends... now why is he here? Is there another secret which is about to get revealed or he was just here for sake of popularity but Arnav is not an attention-seeker kind of a guy.

Oh my god!! What was happening..??? With so many unanswered questions, I left him his friendship in between... I wished I could get back to him, talk to him and clarify things once. And when now I don't need him, I have no feelings for him in my heart –he is right here standing in front of me!! I never ever thought that we would meet again in life. He already had someone in his life whom he was engaged since long time back. Then why was he here??

I looked at him – "Arnav?"

"Thank god you still remember my name!!" He replied with a smile.

"What are you doing here??"-I asked him.

"At least once, you could have asked and discussed things?" –said Arnav.

"What are you talking about!!" I was really worried and shocked to see him there on my event.

"Don't you know Anushree what am I actually talking about...???" he replied.

"Please Arnav go away!! I don't want to talk to you." –I was almost about to cry ... cry, not because I saw Arnav after a long time but I cried out of terror in me of loosing Vivaan...

If Vivaan would see me with Arnav then he would surely get to know the reality of *before saying sorry*.

"I told you Anu, you write really well... and so are you reaping it today!! Congrats..." – he said ignoring my words.

"For what are you here!!! I trusted you!! We were such great friends. At least you would have told me about your girlfriend. Were you that blind that you didn't get an idea that I have started liking you?" – I shouted.

On hearing this, Arnav was actually laughing. He made me sit on the couch and sat down on the floor. He looked into my eyes and said – "Do you really believe that I can lie to you even today?"

His eyes seemed so true. His words were firm.

I ignored looking towards him and said – "What do you want now??"

"I just came here to say that I still love you Anushree... I don't have anyone else in my life!!"

I was numb.

I felt like fainting at that time or becoming invisible or even running away like a mad person. Now this was an actual bomb blast in my life.

Somehow I managed to say – "What??"

And he started –'look Anushree, this is a three year old stuff so there is no point of discussing but with your book I came to know that we both were living in an illusion since long time. Your best friend Haya told me that you like my friend Shikhar and Haya only told you that I am having an affair somewhere else. It was just because Haya was looking for me and Shikhar for you... Haya proposed to me and Shikhar proposed to you after we break-off our friendship. Both of them have planned together to separate us as they could see our chemistry in friendship. But as you didn't have feelings for Shikhar so you refused his proposal and so did I, of Haya!! Our only mistake was that we trusted our friends and so we didn't discuss a thing with each other. You broke our friendship without saying anything. I waited a lot for you. And today we are together again. Just say yes Anushree... I have been literally dying to here this yes from you.'

What the heck was happening right now!! Is this a movie or a television serial? It is my life and I can't handle such pressure on me. In a firm tone I replied – "No!"

He was shocked – "What??"

"No!! when I moved on in life. I realised that whatever I had for you it was just a college crush!! I actually felt what love is, when I met Vivaan." - I said in firm tone.

Arnav angrily said – "Who Vivaan?"

"He is my fiancée. So, there is no point of discussing all this now." – I said.

"Are you really getting married to him?"

"Yes I am.."

"Does he know about me???" –he asked.

"Now why would I tell him about you?" –I replied.

"Does he know anything about your past life?" –he again asked.

"What is your problem Arnav?" –I said in an annoyed tone. I was actually getting annoyed and scared. I was also getting an idea that Arnav's mind is planning something which could be harmful to my and Vivaan's relationship.

"Ohh!! So, he must not be having an idea that your book *before saying sorry* is actually story of your life??" he gave a wicked smile. He really seemed like a villain that time. I never thought that I would see this facc of Arnav. It was hard to believe that this was the same sweet and decent Arnav whom I liked a lot.

Now this was getting serious. Why the hell was he asking me these questions- I wondered.

"What do you want Arnav?" I asked him.

"I want you!! I am going to tell the truth to Vivaan. No guy would marry such a big liar!." – he said and started walking away.

"Wait!! What do you want!! Please why are you ruining my life!! Its all good now. He loves me and I love him. We are getting married. I am sorry if ever I have hurt you. Please forgive me for all my mistake but please don't do this." I requested him.

"No!! lets leave the decision in your Vivaan's hand. Lets tell him the truth and lets see how much he loves you!!!" -He replied.

Now these were heights. My threshold level was reached. Come'on how can any body on earth come to me and threaten me. And how can I be such a coward to get scared with these threats all the time and make wrong decisions. If it was in my destiny, to live all alone without love then fine. I would accept it. But now I would not let any weirdo ruin my life's happiness. I love Vivaan with all my heart and soul. My past life was full of crushes and confusions and also some wrong decisions. And I accept all my mistakes. I will apologize to Vivaan for not telling him the truth of my book. I became selfish as I didn't want to loose Vivaan but now its okay! If its his wish, I will let him go but I will tell him the truth right now.

I ran away without answering to Arnav.

Reached the banquet hall where my event was taking place.

I was searching for Vivaan but could not find him. There were so many people. Everybody was trying to make me talk to them and discuss about the book. But that situation wasn't a chapter of a book. That was my life.

I found Vivaan backstage. He was discussing about how my award would be given to me.

I looked at him and hugged him very tightly. I hugged him as if it was my last hug to him. I was almost in tears.

He asked – "What happened? Are you alright? Are you nervous?"

I was not leaving him and was just crying.

He looked into my eyes and said – "What is it ?"

I said – "I am sorry Vivaan... I love you a lot."

"I love you too Anushree. But why are you crying?" – he replied, wiping my tears from my cheeks.

I because of my sniff was unable to speak a word. He took me outside near the swimming pool. We sat down on a round table. It was just me and him sitting there.

He again asked – "What is it Anu? You alright??"

"Vivaan, do you really like the novel?" – I asked.

"Yes! A lot... so you are actually nervous because of your book. Silly girl!!!" –he laughed and said.

"No!! can I ask something?" –I said.

"Yeah sure!!"

"If I say, the story in that book it wasn't a fiction but was all real. Then?" I questioned.

"Real? Means what?"

"If I say, it was my story and not a word was fictional in that book then!!" – I replied.

"Was it so?" he inquired.

"Yes! It was all true."

He started going away on hearing this.

"Please stop Vivaan!! That day in November, I wanted to give this diary to you. I wanted to tell you all the things through a diary. But I lost that diary. Circumstances were not in the favor of my confession about my past life to you. Many a time I thought of telling you about this book but was unable to... I am really very sorry. Please don't leave me! please don't go!!" I was shouting all this and he was walking away!!

He didn't say a single word. He left me then and there. I was all alone once again.

I really love you Vivaan please don't go!!- I said this to my self with tears running out of my eyes.

I was sitting alone and crying my heart out, meanwhile Arnav came in smiling. I felt like killing him then and there only.

He said – "I am still here for you. I will accept you the way you are."

I turned back to him and said- "Go off you selfish guy. I don't have any feelings for you. Neither of love nor of liking and from now I hate you. I hate you for ruining my life and snatching my Vivaan away from him.

I walked away. Started my car and without letting anyone know, I came to Ganga Bairaj... My most favourite place... The place of my first date with Vivaan...

# 11

# A New Beginning

It had been over 4 hours that I was sitting here all alone looking at the people enjoying their lives. Especially couples.

I never had the pleasure to enjoy like these couples, I always dreamt of roaming around here and there, playing around with no agenda with my fiancée. But my life has something else written for me. Today I lost him. I was all in tears trying to convince myself that whatever I did was absolutely correct.

I would have told him A to Z, very early. His reaction was just perfect. Even if I was in his place, then I would have reacted like him.

But then, I loved him... I wouldn't have left him just like that.

*If god really would have granted me one wish today, then I would just have asked him to forgive me for all my mistakes. Nothing else!!*

My life changed a lot within six hours. Six hours back, I was the centre of attraction, source of pride to many and the most wanted of the city. Now I was all alone. I left the award ceremony. I don't know what must have happened there when they announced my name and found me no-where around.

Vivaan was the only one whom I trusted again with hope that he would never leave me. Will I be able to meet him again? Will I be able to make a best friend and trust her again? Will I be able to live a happy life? What will happen now? -with eyes full of tears, all these thoughts were wandering around my mind...

My mobile was off and I hadn't informed even a single person that I was alone here sitting at the banks of river Ganga...

And by, now... it had started getting dark.

I know it was not safe now for a single girl sitting all by herself at that location but my heart wanted me to stay there till it becomes numb and cries all its pain out.

A small boy interrupted this very personal conversation of mine with myself.

He said - "Didi? Are you crying?"

I replied - "No!!"

And he went away...

After five mintues he returned and again interrupted. He asked - "Didi, how much time more would you be sitting here??"

This small boy of around 10-11 years was actually irritating me.

I said - "Why are you asking all this??"

He replied "that bhaiya told me to..." pointing towards a red i10 car near which Vivaan was standing.

Was he really Vivaan...

He immediately ran towards him.

I was so happy to see him. I wanted to hug him but... I controlled myself and said – "Why are you here now??"

"What???" –he said.

"You left me... you broke our relation off... now go!!!!" – I shouted at him.

"If I really would have left you then I would not have been standing behind you waiting for you to turn back, since last 2.5 hours.."

On hearing this I burst out into tears and hugged him very tightly.

I cried – "I was really scared. I thought now I will never ever see you again. I felt the feeling of loosing someone today. Promise me you will never ever leave me again???"

He replied – "I love you Anushree... that time I wasn't sure how to react so went away for sometime to calm myself down".

"But how come you came to know that I was here??" I asked Vivaan as it was a surprise to see Vivaan there as I hadn't informed anyone that I would come here...

"Remember Anu, on our first date you told me that you love this place... it is the most favourite place of yours in the whole world and you like to come here whenever you are happy or sad or you want to be alone..."

I couldn't control bursting into tears again when I heard this. I was running short of words... or rather should say I could not speak because I was crying...

"And see what I have brought for you." said Vivaan pointing inside the car's window.

"What??" -said me.

He took out my award from his car's front seat and handed it over to me.

This moment really took my breath away for a few seconds. I was looking on that precious award in my hands.

"You know what? Your mom received this award and gave a brilliant speech on your behalf." -He said.

But I was silent...

Vivaan said - "Anushree?"

I replied - "Yes?"

He said - "You know what? I am really proud of you. You by now really have the courage to accept the truth. You told your story to the whole world. Now I not only love you but respect you a lot. Thank you for being in my life... I love you!!!"

"I love you too Vivaan......................................"

P.S. : And they lived happily ever after!

Warning: Don't mess with the flow of life, it can really make your life ***too hard to handle***...